Twisted Tales

of the

Yellow Brick Road

by
A. Yasin

Dedication

To Mom and Dad,

You're awesome.

And though you don't read fantasy, this one's for you anyway.

(On second thoughts, don't read it. It'll make for awkward conversation at the dinner table.)

Table of Contents

Acknowledgement

Thank you to all the English teachers who put up with me and forgave my less-than-focused self in class, time and time again. I was paying attention, I promise, and this is proof. Sort of.

A huge thank you to Terry, without whom I probably would not have finished this anthology, never mind gotten around to make it presentable for publishing. You have been an invaluable help.

Thank you ever so much to Val, my best friend and my biggest supporter in every writing venture I've embarked upon. I second guess myself a lot but your encouragement has never failed to work.

Thank you to Aqsa and Namra, the cheerleaders I don't deserve. I've always promised I would publish something and put you in the acknowledgements. Here's me fulfilling my promise because you absolutely deserve it.

And lastly, thank you to my parents for not forcing me to be an engineer, doctor or lawyer. Thank you for swallowing any misgivings you might have had and allowing me to choose my own path. It means a lot.

VIII

Preface

Fairy tales do not normally require a warning. These ones do.

Not suitable for children

Golden Eyes

Part I

Stray not beyond the village wall,

For the woods are dark,

and the night is long.

Beware, beware,

The Goblin King's call.

A *saying as old as time. Or so her village elders would have her believe. But the young girl's mind was frivolous. The cobwebs of common sense did not anchor her as they did those who were older and wiser. She saw no merit in their sayings. The young girl did what the young girl wanted.*

Now this precocious young woman had a name once. But much time had passed since it had been used last, and even she had forgotten what it was. Rather, she wore the moniker given to her by her grandmother: Golden Eyes. For her orbs were as her name implied. They were bright and fiery, as if the sun had shed a tear and then another, letting both fall into the hollows of her skull. They festered there, so lovely, so bright.

Golden Eyes had disobeyed her elders yet again this fine morning. But not for the usual reasons. She had not dabbed rouge on her cheeks and lips. And she certainly had not brought a pretty scarf to tie her hair back with. And she had not spent her hard-earned money on new shoes. Oh no, this time, Golden Eyes bore the intention of doing something worse. Had her grandmother found out, she would have cuffed Golden Eyes to her wrist and beaten her bloody.

No one noticed the young girl slip through a side gate, straight towards the forbidden woods. The guard in the watchtower had had his sweetheart pay him a visit. They were wrapped in a tangle of arms and legs, frantically working their way towards a babe in the crib nine months later. Neither would be glad for it when winter came and pinched its little toes to make it squeal.

Oh, the grass was softer here! Her small feet made no sound as she rushed across it. It was as verdant as she. She ran as if she was escaping the Devil himself. But the smile on her face was godly. Clouds drew themselves closer, covering the cerulean sky and casting shadows over her bright face. It was as if they warned her:

Do not laugh so loud and dance so light!

Lest you attract the Goblin King's blight!

Golden Eyes heeded no call. She twirled and leapt, skirts billowing, hair flying, arms flailing. The trees leaned towards her, stretching their bony arms and grabbing at her. She ran to them without a care. Their branches hung low – they were alive. They tore her skirts into tatters, they left seeds and rotten leaves in her hair, whispering after her: "Your scent belies your youth, little one! He sees you!"

Golden Eyes spoke not the language of the trees. She pulled twigs off her sleeves and kicked a rock out of her way and laughed scornfully. For a moment, she almost believed the woods were trying to imprison her. But how could one so wild and free be imprisoned by those chained to the austere earth?

Golden Eyes failed to notice the kiss of summer had not reached the woods. With the barest of leaves and the spindliest of branches, they were destitute and they were desperate. She noticed not their creaking screams and mangled limbs. She wanted more, more, more, she wanted to know everything there was to know about this land she had never been allowed to wander.

Golden Eyes trespassed on the land but failed to acknowledge its ruler.

He, however, acknowledged her.

Her ceaseless exploration halted for a split second. What was this she heard? Larks? And so many! No, not just larks, but birds of all shapes and voices! Golden Eyes cocked her head and listened. They were towards the west. Her feet trod carefully now, afraid she would disturb this lovely menagerie, wherever it was.

A cluster of branches, dense undergrowth, a rock that stabbed through the sole of her shoe and then she emerged out onto a glade. Golden Eyes forgot the agony in her foot and her jaw dropped.

A menagerie indeed. There they were. Hundreds of birds – larks, robins, crows, nightingales – sharing the same imprisonment. The trees were taller here, their branches sturdier. Hanging from them were iron wrought cages and inside, sat the birds, weeping tears made of ice. They sparkled, brazen diamonds in the sunlight. The rays of the sun trickled through leafy shamrocks, creating golden ropes of heat; each tear sparkled against them, a precious jewel on a gold chain, before fizzling out. Golden Eyes caught one just as it melted. It kissed her hot palm and evaporated in the blink of an eye.

The keening trill of a flute cut the air. The birds were silenced and the trees became still. Golden Eyes felt her lungs refuse to obey her. They would not draw breath and oh, she couldn't bear it! She clutched her chest, her throat, falling to her knees. She wanted to return to the village. She wanted to hug her grandmother and promise to never disobey her again. She wished, she hoped she would be able to do so before her life drained from her.

Just when Golden Eyes thought she could feel Death's keen, cold scythe lick at her neck, her chest expanded. Her first breath was stumbling, awkward. It hurt almost as much as not having it. Then, she was a new born again and she rediscovered the use of her lungs. She sucked at Mother Nature's teat for air and received it in abundance. Once she was able, she dragged herself up on her feet, meaning to run back to the village and beg her grandmother's forgiveness.

But her exit from the glade was barred, for there stood the Goblin King.

She rightly mistook him for a tree at first. In fact, he was meshed into three trees, his limbs theirs and his skin their bark. But then he shrunk and the moss faded as did the coarse *edges of the bark. He became human, but yet not so human after all. Tall, he was so tall. And as terrifying and as beautiful as a thunderstorm in summer. A creature of nightmares, lurking in the shadows of the glade.*

She backed away into a small pool of sunlight; it drew a halo on her wild curls and warmed the blades of her shoulders as if preparing them for the sprouting of magnificent wings. Wings she could use to fly away and escape. But alas, this was the Goblin King's abode and he controlled all the entryways and the exits. There was no escape.

"Do you fear me, child?"

His voice was nothing more than a whisper but it held within it all the notes of a pan flute. Earthy, lustful and husky. The earth itself had spoken. It restored humanity to his features and some of her fear drained from her veins.

He continued to tower over her but the twigs that made up his hair slackened, softer and silkier now. They blanched of all colour from the roots, becoming whiter than the snow which had not settled on the land for many months now. It fell down his back one moment and fluttered on the back of an unfelt, unheard wind the next. His skin was as dark as the trunk of a cedar tree and his eyes as green as the sun sprayed leaves above him. But they were acidic. Poison. His eyes were a beautiful poison and they invited her to drink.

If the Tree of Knowledge had ever taken human form, the Goblin King was he.

His clothes were not like hers at all. Leaves of all different shades hung about his waist, dyed red, gold and green, forming a drape around his shoulders and rustling against the white wisps of his hair. His fingers clenched and she could swear she heard them creak like tired branches; they were long and tapered and her imagination went wild. They could wrap all the way around her slim neck and crush the life out of her as easily as a beetle's.

He frightened her.

"Once he has you, he keeps you. He destroys you, he skins you, he leaves you out to dry. The Goblin King is worse, much worse than the devils of old."

Golden Eyes felt tears freeze and then fall from her ducts. Small, hard pebbles tumbling down her cheeks, sparkling and precious. Her tears were ice. Her breath became a cloud. Her limbs trembled. The sunlight was gone and darkness swallowed the forest. The birds began to sing, crying out their little hearts. The anxiety of the caged prisoners was palpable. They feared for her. They cried for her.

Muffling them all, the Goblin King's laughter rattled the glade.

Sleeping Ugly

*O*n a beautiful summers day, a winding yellow brick road was traversed by the muted knocking of a horse's hooves. The horse itself moved at a pondering speed. Whilst it catches up, for the sake of our tale, let us admire the portrait of serenity Mother Nature graced us with that morning.

On either side of the road, stretched meadows peppered with yellow buttercups. Their colour was so uncannily similar to the bricks, it was as if a million such buttercups had been crushed to their deaths to give the road its perfect shade. To the east stretched woods as far as the naked eye could see, tall solemn soldiers with green helmets and grim dispositions. These woods were widely known as being haunted by many a dark and evil creature, and ruled over by the fearsome Erl King. How fortunate then, that this tale has nothing to do with him or them.

A white stallion came prancing into view, his mane rippled and his tail swung. Powerful muscles rippled under his silky coat; he was bred from prize winning parents and was built for hardier tasks. But he was content with the one he had and carried his prince on his back with pride.

Whether by vain accident or otherwise, the handsome young Prince was dressed in white and gold livery. He and his horse made quite the colour coordinated pair. The Prince appeared to be thoroughly enjoying the fine day, running his hand through his flaxen hair. He was incredibly proud of its thick, glossy weight and had had it freshly curled just that morning.

He had travelled a long way to find this road. Very long indeed. And now that he could see the turrets of a castle in the distance, he felt his purpose strengthen.

This land once belonged to a King and Queen who had ruled for many a year. They had had only one daughter, a famed beauty (but very few people had ever seen her) and the future heir to the throne. Alas, upon her birth, a witch cast a curse on the child and though no one knew exactly what it entailed, it took effect on her sixteenth birthday. Unclimbable walls of briar rose grew around the castle at unnatural speeds on that day, sealing the fate of the people inside. No one had yet managed to get through and see what had become of them.

Many had attempted it. Their well-meaning bones now furnished the brambles.

Just a short distance from the first layer of hedges sat a wizened old man. He looked to be a beggar, hunched under monk's robes with a cauldron by his side. He had a pack of belongings and from the top peeked a sturdy sword hilt. It was a strange thing for a beggar to own. He held out his tanned, leathery hands to the Prince, pleading for money.

The Prince ran his hand through his golden locks and pretended he hadn't heard. Instead, he studied the sky, humming pleasantly. Up above, the smoke trails of a witch's broomstick cut through the undiluted blue of the heavens. What a marvellous sight.

Upon reaching the briar rose hedges, the Prince dismounted and unsheathed his sword. He went at it immediately, confident he would get through in no time. He was special. He was not like the others who had come before him. He was a prince and he could do anything!

But his sword was too elegant and was made for polite jabs during a fencing match, with plenty of breaks for tea. It did not hold a chance. The only thing the Prince managed to dislodge was a skull (much to his horror). Now, he was no longer so optimistic. His face was red and his perfect locks mussed. The sun was starting to lower in the sky and he feared he would not be through by nightfall.

The beggar was still by the roadside. The Prince recalled the pack he had had lying beside him. It held inside it what was most certainly a sturdier sword than his.

"My good fellow, what may I offer you in return for that marvellous sword of yours?"

The old man eyed him, muttering under his breath. Out loud, he said, "I begged for a few coins earlier. Had you provided me with them then, I might have gone to town and brought a pie to eat. Now I sit here hungry and the market is closed."

"Come, come, once I've fulfilled my mission I will treat you to the finest meal my kingdom has to offer. You will be showered in gold for your services."

"Your empty promises are like cobwebs to my hungry belly. I will accept nothing less than your entire kingdom in exchange for my sword."

And with that, the beggar gathered up his pack, for he was tired and the town's many alleyways would make safer lodging than the open skies above the yellow brick road. The Prince watched him totter away, barely able to hold his pack on his hunched back.

"Let me make your load lighter, my friend."

He drew forward and lifted his own sword. It was no good for the tangled hedges but it very easily cut the beggar from ear to ear. The cracks in the yellow bricks bled scarlet and the Prince took the old man's sword with him.

It worked as if it was enchanted. Indeed, the Prince wondered how such a vagrant had gotten his hands on such a weapon. It cut the hedges like butter and it was not long before the Prince was on the other side.

He wasted no time in making his way up to the castle. Here and there, lay servants of all ranks and ages. It appeared when the curse had hit, it had taken everyone by surprise. Everyone had fallen where they stood and had slept deeply for a hundred years. Not a single one had turned into dust. Except for an abnormal growth of facial hair in the case of the men, they all remained unchanged.

The Prince searched every room. It was no easy task. There were hundreds. He scoured and searched until finally he reached the last and highest tower. Up, up, up he went, dizzy by the time he reached the top. He sank against the wall by a small niche window to catch his breath.

And that was when he saw her.

A maid was snoring softly outside the door to the only room in the tower. She was dressed in a drab dress and dirty apron, her cap askew and her shoes grubby. She was dumpy, with a hooked nose and thin lips. Mousey brown hair hung from under her cap like wispy threads. There was no telling her age. She could have been very old or very young.

"What a hideous creature," the Prince murmured.

He nudged her with his foot. When that did not work, he pushed, heaving her away from the door. She rolled like a sack of potatoes and her snoring was silenced. From her pocket, rolled a spool of thread with a small needle attached to it.

The door hid behind it an enchanting boudoir, fragranced and decorated with roses. Silk hung from the windows and garlands of flowers dangled from the candelabra. Ivy was growing wild, covering the walls and floor and the bed in the centre of the room.

It was set on a dais, covered by a canopy of curtains. And on it lay the most beautiful princess the Prince had ever laid eyes on. Her hair was as golden as his, her lips were a delicate pink and she was wearing a gown of pure white. She looked perfect, a serene bride on her wedding night. Out of all the people the

Prince had seen so far, she was the only one who did not look like she had been caught unawares.

"She must have known her horrible fate was drawing nigh. Oh, sweet girl…" he murmured, a poignant longing in his voice as he drew close.

He wished he could stare at her forever. But the urge to kiss her grew, until finally, he bent down and placed his lips on hers. He half expected her to wake and kiss him back. No such luck. Her chest continued to rise and fall steadily, her eyes tightly closed.

The Prince decided that since he had solved the first hurdle of getting through to the castle, the curse could be dealt with by others. The princess he was determined to marry and he was sure that there was many a skilled mage in his land who could lift the spell off of her. Once she was awake, he would tell her there had been no way of saving the others for they had become dusty bones. Only she had remained whole.

After all, when the King of this land had fallen asleep, the Prince's grandfather had quickly conquered it. It would not bode well for their empire for the old rulers to awaken again.

And so, the Prince loaded the sleeping princess onto his stallion and rode day and night until he reached his own castle. But try as they might, all the mages in the land could not revive her. She remained asleep, sweet and demure and unknowing. A year passed and the Prince could not bear it any longer.

"I must marry her," he declared to his parents.

Though they found their son's request strange, they did not wish to deal with his tantrums and agreed.

It was a fairy tale wedding. Dignitaries and royals from all the other kingdoms were invited. Food and drink was aplenty in the land, largess was scattered at every street corner and the festivities went on for a month and one day. It was such an expensive wedding, most people completely forgot the bride was asleep through it all.

That did not deter her eager husband.

Another year passed and still buried in a deep sleep, the princess gave birth to their first child. The King and Queen were overjoyed and declared a public holiday in honour of their first grandson.

Now, as it happened, the King had recently appointed a clever young man to the post of Master of the Treasury. The new treasurer had worked his way up from nothing and was extremely well-mannered and very adept at his job. He was valued in the King's parliament for his quick thinking and astute policies.

The Treasurer had recently taken it upon himself to investigate the casting of the Sleeping Curse, as it was now known. Something itched inside him, a feeling of guilt and shame. Would this land have a Sleeping Queen once the Prince became King? It was not fair that she should spend such a life, oblivious to her child and her kingdom. He also believed it was not fair that a royal of her calibre be carted like a sack of goods across the land to be married off without her knowledge. But to voice such an opinion would have been to commit treason.

So, the Treasurer continued his studies in silence. As it so happened, he discovered an interesting fact of history in a dusty old tome. The princess born to the neighbouring kingdom had had a birthmark behind her ear. There was nothing pertaining to the details of the witch's curse or examples of other curses cast in a similar fashion. Nothing towards finding a cure. Nothing to unravel the mystery that she was. Just a strawberry mark.

To satisfy his curiosity, the Treasurer decided to see if the birthmark existed.

The princess was laid out in state in a grand bedroom on the fourth floor of the castle. Since she had arrived, not a finger on either of her hands had ever twitched. Once her guards heard he had a possible solution to the princess's curse, they allowed him entry. They only assumed they were doing the right thing. With a thudding heart, the young man entered the room.

He had only been there for half a minute when the Prince entered.

"Your Highness!" the Treasurer whirled around.

The Prince was furious that he had been allowed inside and demanded to know what he was up to. The Treasurer stammered, explaining that he was only attempting to serve His Royal Highness as best he could. But before he could say another word, the Prince held his hand up for silence.

"You are valued by my father and you are a man of great intelligence and honour. Therefore, I will be merciful in retribution to your heinous offence. You are hereby banished from this kingdom. Never set foot in it again!"

The Prince would hear no more and the Treasurer was banished accordingly. By the time the King heard of his son's decision, it was far too late. He was furious and demanded

that his prized official be returned but the
Treasurer was nowhere to be found. It appeared
he truly had left the kingdom.

He was now in search of the famed
yellow brick road.

And thus, we once again return to a
familiar scene.

There the castle came into view and there
by the side of the road, sat the wizened old
beggar looking quite alive and well. The
Treasurer gave him half of what he had left in
his purse and moved on. The hedges had
regrown where the Prince had cut them apart
and try as he might, the Treasurer could not
perform a similar feat. It was then that the old
beggar offered him his broad sword.

It worked like magic.

There were many females in the castle
but the young man checked behind the ear of
each and every one. Nothing was as it seemed,
a lesson he had learned well. Finally, he
retraced the Prince's steps all the way up to the
tower room. It now lay empty but there was
one last person lying in the shadows. It was the
young maid.

He bent down and lifted a spool of
thread, stabbed through with a needle. It must
have rolled out of her apron pocket, he thought.

He gently lifted her, sitting her up against the wall. Then, he took off her cap and swept her hair back off her forehead.

And there it was.

A small strawberry shaped mark behind her ear.

For a moment, the Treasurer was speechless and his mind went blank. It was the Princess herself! There was no doubt about it. But for the life of him, he could not understand why she was in such a state. And who was it that was now married to the Prince of his land?

The longer he looked at her, splinters formed in his heart, threatening to break it. It was such a terrible fate for such a harmless, young girl. She looked quite plain in her maid's garb but despite having lain in one place for a hundred and one years, her cheeks were rosy red. It gave her an air of sweet innocence. Tears formed in his eyes.

"I am so sorry I can't help you, my lady," he whispered.

Then, he leant down and pressed a kiss on her forehead. As he did, a tear fell from his eye and rolled down his cheek, landing on her long lashes. It glistened there, a trembling dewdrop and then it slid down her face, disappearing under her chin.

Her breath quickened. One gasp, then a second. And then she was breathing as if she had run a very long distance to reach consciousness.

One by one, the sleepers in the castle began to awake. In the neighbouring land, the Prince received the greatest shock of his life when his wife suddenly sat up and began to scream in terror, having no idea where she was and being completely distraught at finding a half-naked stranger beside her.

It was a tale that was retold many a time after its main players were long dead.

At her christening ceremony, a most evil witch had cursed the Princess to prick her finger on a needle and sleep till the end of days. Her concerned parents had gotten rid of all the needles and spinning wheels in the land, not wanting to risk their precious daughter's safety.

The Princess was confined to the castle and became very lonely. Her only friend was a maid who served her, a beautiful young woman who had grown up with the Princess. They often amused themselves by exchanging clothes and play acting as if their statuses were also swapped. However, unbeknownst to the Princess, as her friend lay on her bed and daydreamed about how splendid it would be to have been born royal, there was a spool of thread and a needle the maid had forgotten in her apron pockets. It had only taken a brief slip of the Princess's hand for the curse to take effect and she fell to the ground, unconscious.

And so, a particularly strange series of events was set into motion.

The King and Queen rewarded the Treasurer by knighting him and giving him a hundred times his weight in gold. Once they heard his story, he was given the familiar role of Master of the Treasury and he proved very efficient in managing the state's coffers during the war to retake the kingdom from its conquerors. It was won within three years and the land rejoiced. The Princess was by this time deeply in love with the shy, studious young man and he was very much enamoured with her.

They were married and became King and Queen not long after, ruling over a golden age for their kingdom.

As for the Prince and his wife…

Well, there is one twist to this story that both the Princess and the Treasurer remained oblivious to.

The witch who had cast the curse had a daughter, a pretty young thing with a mind as sharp as her mother's. It would no doubt have broken the Princess's heart to learn that her best friend, the maid, had been planted by her side from a young age. After all, what a coincidence for there to be no needles in the land except one, lodged deep in the pocket of a mere castle maid.

The Prince in the neighbouring kingdom decided not to exile his young wife. She was not at fault, he summarised and besides, she was the most beautiful woman in the land and everyone who saw her agreed. Their story does go on and has quite the nasty end, of which you shall hear in due time.

I hear you ask of the beggar: Who was he? Where did he come from? Didn't he die?

Well, I'm afraid I just don't know about all that.

Golden Eyes

Part II

"Will you drink with me,
Golden Eyes?"

His voice trembled through the glade like the first arctic wind of winter. The sun was a faded dream, its heat no longer protecting her. All around, the icy tears of the caged birds hailed down upon her like pebbles. They pricked her skin, a thousand little needles of spite. Golden Eyes cowered. Her own tears ripped her ducts as they burst out, as hard and as icy as the ones falling on her.

"Why do you cry, child?"

Frozen eyelids struggled to blink as she turned, searching for him. He had disappeared, leaving only his voice behind as a mournful echo. Sad. He sounded so unbearably sad. Golden eyes reached out with trembling fingers, blinded by her own tears.

"I-I cannot see. My tears are made of ice," she moaned.

He laughed and with the resounding, clear notes, the sunlight returned. Golden Eyes *could see again. Her tears were no longer pebbles of frozen water. They melted and made her cheeks damp. She laughed, in relief and delight, wiping her face. When she turned, she saw that the clearing was now larger and the birds in their cages were nowhere to be seen. Joy filled her heart as she saw a house made of earth and thatched with a roof of leaves. What a dear little house it was! Her panic was quite forgotten.*

It was spacious and filled with the refreshing scent of loam. There was nothing else inside, except for a singular bed made of birch wood and canopied with green ivy. At the other end, a small cauldron hung in the hearth, bubbling with the most marvellous aromas. What it could possibly be cooking, baffled her. For she saw no vegetables, no spice racks or racks of meat anywhere. The cauldron simply stirred itself, all the while conjuring up that wonderful smell.

A shadow cast over the floor, blocking the sun. Golden Eyes turned, as nervous as a rabbit in a trap. Fear flashed in her eyes for the barest of seconds. And then it melted to be replaced with glee. Her full lips curved into an innocuous smile and she laughed. Laughter certainly came easily to her.

"What is it that you are cooking? Is it rabbit? Or deer? Or perhaps one of those birds? Is that why you had them in cages?" she asked.

The Goblin King chuckled, shaking his head as he walked to the bed. "Sweet child, such things are forbidden for me to eat."

"But why? You are their ruler. You rule these woods, do you not? Everything is yours to have."

"One who rules must never devour his own subjects. For what would there be left to rule? Save for nights filled with stomach upsets and misery."

He clasped his hands and when they parted, a cloak coloured a most magnificent shade of vermilion materialised between them. Golden Eyes was aghast, for his magic frightened her as much as it delighted the parts of her inclined towards the mystical and unknown. Forwards she drew, and his green eyes never left her visage, painting her with the keen amusement of his glance. He looked at her sometimes as if she were but a child and yet the cloak –

The cloak, oh the cloak.

When he put it around her shoulders, the touch of his hands stirred a feeling so abrupt, so profound, Golden Eyes faltered for a moment, unsure what to do. The Goblin King spun her around and the poignant emerald of his eyes told her all that she needed to know.

And it was wonderful.

Golden Eyes forgot how long she remained in the Goblin King's realm. She changed. Her hair was wilder, strung with the deep green leaves she now wore over her body. And atop it all, the scarlet cloak she always wore, for it was his gift and she held it dear. She was so happy.

His little Queen, he called her, always with a hint of mockery. Never enough to offend, but just enough to beguile. She felt very young when he was near, that was true. She was porcelain in his large hands, so easily ruined should he let her fall. But always, he held tight. Golden Eyes wore his red cloak to bed, refusing to loosen it even as he tore the leaves from her body and left her bare.

The nights were the longest, the darkest, full of both delights and terror. Often, she would hear the silvery, whispered cries of a thousand forlorn birds, pelting her with ominous warnings. She wondered where all the cages had disappeared to but whenever she was about to ask, the Goblin King's lips wiped her mind clean, fickle slate that it was.

*Content to be his wife by breathless
confirmations of love and by flesh, Golden
Eyes wandered the forest as if in a dream.
Days passed…or were they months? Years?
Centuries? She knew not the haunting clasp of
Time's embrace but with it, she forgot its
trustworthiness.*

*Golden Eyes told the Goblin King
nothing of it, but she was in search of the birds.*

*Something inside her, as carefree and
blithe as she was, urged her to find the
feathered prisoners. They hid something of
great importance and she had to know it, she
just had to! And Golden Eyes was nothing if
not resourceful.*

*The Goblin King had conjured her a pair
of ruby red shoes to match her velveteen cloak.
One day, she put them on and she set off,
determined to find the edge of the forest. Many
times, she had attempted this venture, but her
mind wandered, distracting her by will or by
force, and she was diverted.*

*Golden Eyes ran through the clawing,
greedy trees, much like she had run into their
embrace the day she met the Goblin King.
Faster and faster, the wind blew against her
back, thrusting her ever forward. As she ran,
her shoes got tighter and tighter, becoming hot
like coals. She shrieked in pain, but her mind*

cleared and she knew it was some heinous mischief of the Goblin King's. The shoes were laced with enchantment and she, the poor fly, trapped in the web.

The last few yards, Golden Eyes crawled. Her nails dug into the soil, dragging her forward. For the shoes ached so and she could not bear it. But what marvel! Once she had crossed the threshold of the forest and the last tree recoiled its knobbly branches from her leg, the shoes no longer tormented her.

She found that she could stand, she could walk, she could run!

Golden Eyes ran, sobbing with such emotion. It was neither good nor bad, but it was powerful. How she yearned to lay eyes on her poor old grandmother!

The village walls were higher now and there was another sentry tower beside the first. Both were manned by guards who seemed not to hear her call. In a futile effort, Golden Eyes tried to open a side gate. The latch lifted and she laughed in girlish delight, meaning to slip through.

But oh horror!

She could not pass. A barrier pushed her away, an invisible wall of steel that disallowed her from entering. Golden Eyes sobbed, trying all in her power to push past. It was to no avail. Again, she screamed to the guards, at the top of her voice. But they did not hear her. They could not hear her. For Golden Eyes had left the land of mortals far behind and she was no longer one of them.

Sinking to her knees, the young girl cried, watering the plush soil with tears that seemed to have no end. From each one sprouted a white lily until she sat in a pool of glowing white. High above, the guards watched in amazement, for they saw no explanation for such a miracle. Lily upon lily sprang from the barren soil, growing at unnatural speed.

Golden Eyes turned her feet back to the only home she now had. She would have quite passed it had she not turned to gaze longingly at her village one last time. But there, in a field filled with bright yellow flowers, was the wooden marker of a grave.

Her grave. Her empty grave.

And then it was that she saw she had been proclaimed dead for many a year now. To the people of the village, she was but a scrap of history, buried in the field she loved to play in the most as a simple village girl. Shaking hands touched the wooden pole, tracing the carvings upon it as brimming, doe eyes refused to believe what they saw.

Dead.

The Goblin King's cursed enchantments were nothing before the dooming finality of her grave. Golden Eyes turned her back on it with a frail sob, her red shoes forcing her to return from whence she had come. What awaited her was not home. She had no home. She was but a wild, orphan waif, at the mercy of a wily and menacing ruler.

"Once he has you, he keeps you. He destroys you, he skins you, he leaves you out to dry. The Goblin King is worse, much worse than the devils of old."

Onwards, she went, hunting out his lair and the longer she walked, the foggier her memories got. She forgot the grave, the village, her life. Her tears dried and a fervent, chattering laugh slipped from her lips. She began to dance, carefree again. Except something was not right.

For no matter how long she searched, in every nook, cranny and clearing, Golden Eyes could not find the Goblin King's hut. No bird song, no rumbling laugh, no bubbling cauldron —

He was gone.

Cinder

So, there was this rat –
My apologies. Let me start again.

*O*nce upon a time, there lived a rat. Let not the word stir revulsion in your gut, for this rat was a delicate, fragile little creature. More of a gentrified, lady-like mouse than a rat, really. Her coat was made of the silkiest, pale grey fur, her eyes were large and bright and such whiskers! Not a finer set of whiskers could be found in all the land.

This particular rat – we shall call her Cinder due to her place of residence in the hearth of a cellar – was special for more than just her rodential beauty. She was a rat only in appearance, or so she told herself. The life she would have chosen for herself was far different. She looked down upon her compatriots, who often went scavenging in the humans' pantry for food. She adamantly refused to do the same which led to her malnourished state. Often the other rats took pity on her and suggested an exchange of their food scraps for one of the tiny trinkets she had stolen from the jewellery boxes of the humans upstairs. Anything to make her eat. They found her habits baffling; to them, stealing glass beads was scavenging also. But Cinder had a very short temper if her principles were questioned, so no one dared argue.

Poor Cinder. All her short life she had wished to be born human. She had seen the beds of silk and down, the plush rugs and the fancy furnishings of the house above, and it tugged at her heartstrings. She also wished to dance around in gowns that swept the floor, merry and light. The laughter of the two merchant's daughters could often be heard in her little hearth through the chimney. She fell asleep at night hearing the soft thrumming of their delicate voices, gossiping late into the night.

And when she slept, oh what dreams she had!

Cinder dreamt she was the ruler of the humans and her ball gowns were the biggest and brightest of all. Her hair would be silky grey like her fur and she would have the biggest, darkest eyes. Whomsoever looked at her would fall for her enigmatic charms, and yet no one would fully understand her. Cinder liked being a mystery. She was a mystery to her fellow rats but it was not their timid fascination she required.

Cinder had tried to make friends with the two sisters on more than one occasion. Both times their shrieks had deafened her and the second time she had almost been kicked to death by their housekeeper. She had barely escaped with her life through a hole in the skirting one of her brothers had gnawed through the previous week.

Poor Cinder never attempted such a foolhardy mission again. Instead, she hid in that small, dark hole and spied on the sisters as they went about their whimsical, glittering lives.

Today, they were very excited. Between them, they were trying to scan the contents of a scroll but were unable to as one would snatch it and then the other. Their mother came bustling in, scolding them for creating such an ungodly racket.

"Young ladies, I am appalled at this churlish behaviour! Get yourselves together at once! Mitsy, where is the letter from the palace? Bitsy, do you have it? I see it! Don't try and hide it!"

"Oh mother, you won't believe it!" Bitsy squealed, prancing up and down and tittering, much like a mare in heat.

"You won't believe it, you *won't*!" Mitsy parroted in her nasal little voice.

"What? Hand it over," their mother commanded, proceeding to put on her lorgnette and frown at the scroll.

In flashes, her face turned white, then red, then a slightly mellow pink. Then puce and then such an alarming shade of beetroot, Cinder thought she was sure to witness her first human death. But instead, the mother began to jump up and down much like her daughters (except this time, Cinder felt the floor quake and her tiny body shook with it).

"My goodness! Girls! This is it! Our fortune is made! You will both go to the ball and whichever one the prince falls in love with, she will be princess and then – and then she will be *queen*! Oh, hail to the Goddess! We are saved!"

"It's going to be me," Bitsy said immediately. For further clarification, she added, "Me. He's going to pick me."

"Oh tosh! He'll choose me!" Mitsy announced, puffing out her chest. "The size of my bosom is considerably greater than yours. I *told* you to rub castor oil into them. They're the size of raisins!"

She proceeded to snicker cruelly to which her sister took much offence.

"Yes, well your behind could comfortably seat ten people, so who's *really* losing here?" Bitsy snorted.

The sisters launched themselves at each other, screeching like rabid manatees. Their mother did not even notice. She was in hysterics over the scroll, imagining all kinds of wild future scenarios in which she would be addressed as the 'Queen Mother' and dine only on solid gold plates.

Cinder could not bear to watch the stomach-turning scene much longer. She turned tail and slunk back into the darkness, her heart heavy.

"As if the prince would choose such vile creatures to sit on his throne beside him," she grumbled to herself, "I've not seen this prince but I know that he must be handsome. He is obviously rich. He would go for nothing but the crème de la crème of his female subjects. Alas! If only I had been born human, what fun I would have at the ball! I would catch his eye from across the room, making him quite lose his mind. In a trance, he would come to me and ask 'My lady, forgive me, but I was losing hope of ever finding a bride having seen the large, but lacklustre selection of candidates my kingdom has thus far provided. But upon seeing your face…by the Goddess, I think I am bewitched. I will settle for nothing less but your hand in marriage.' And then I would chuckle sweetly – behind my glove of course, for to show my teeth would be so unladylike – and would say, "Your Highness! At least ask me to dance first!" And then he would laugh and everyone and their mothers would seethe in jealousy as we dance until our feet are blistered and bleeding. Oh, if only I were human…"

And thus, Cinder wove another fantasy and for a few blissful moments, forgot her base position in life as she allowed her heartbeat to quicken.

The cold, damp hearth welcomed her back to reality and she slept on her pillow of cinders that night, crying silently.

No, the story does not end here.

The next morning, quite early even for her usual time, Cinder woke to the sound of a plaintive little voice calling for help. Her body ached from head to tail and the sound was so far away. Not close enough to bother about, surely. But Cinder was a kind rat and it certainly sounded as if the owner of the voice was in dire straits.

She followed the sound, wriggling through the gap in the cellar window and out onto the street. The alleyway was quiet and up above, the stars trembled in anticipation of the approaching sun. Cinder frantically searched as the voice began to lapse into screams. At last, she saw a large rat, sniffing at something behind the dustbins. She bounded over, thinking one of her brethren was in trouble. But when he saw her, he grunted, "Look! Breakfast!"

Cinder peeked around the bin and gasped in horror. A small fairy was trapped behind a brick, wailing in devastation as she stared into the gaping maw of the much bigger rat. Cinder jumped into action immediately and promptly bit him on his behind.

"How dare you try to eat the poor little thing! Be gone with you!" she squeaked, biting him again.

Now though this rat was much bigger, he was a little slow in the head. And Cinder was so very pretty, and he had *such* a soft spot for her, that he did not wish to turn her against him. He had been stocking up on grain all summer in preparation for the harsh winter months and one day, he hoped to present it to her as he asked her to be his mate. In sight of this future, he backed away, apologised to both ladies and scampered back into the cellar.

"I am so sorry. He's such a dolt. We're not all like this, I assure you," Cinder said. "However did you get yourself into such a predicament?"

The fairy had been momentarily stunned into silence upon hearing such eloquent speech from a rat. Then, she remembered her manners and cleared her throat, bowing to her saviour.

"I lost a ring of mine around here and I returned to look for it. But as I was doing so, that – that *rat* came and began pushing the brick against the wall so I would be trapped and he could eat me! I don't know what I would have done if you hadn't shown up! Thank you so much…?"

"Cinder," the female rat simpered. "You're very welcome. It would be such a shame if a pretty little thing like you were to be eaten by such an ugly brute. Come, let me help you out."

The fairy was still doubtful of the rat's good intentions. She suspected that Cinder's kindness was a ploy and that she would gobble her up quicker than her wings could flutter and carry her away. But once Cinder had her out, she began to gently dust off the fairy's wings with her tail and fussing over the minor scratches and bruises she'd suffered.

In fact, the fairy was so full of gratitude, she decided to grant Cinder a wish.

"There isn't enough I can do to repay you for saving my life. But I would like to start by using some of my magic dust to grant you a wish, dear Cinder," she said.

Cinder was gobsmacked. She could hardly breathe for excitement! She twirled round and round, squeaking frantically before breathlessly falling against the wall.

"I-I do have a wish! Oh, I do! I-I wish – I wish – "

"Take a deep breath – and another – and now speak," the fairy instructed.

Cinder did as she said and she found she could breathe again. Her words came tumbling out, one on top of the other.

"I wish to be human for a night so that I may go to the ball and meet the prince!"

In her heart of hearts, Cinder believed this wish to be so impossible, that she did not think the fairy with her magic dust could actually manage it. But much to her astonishment, the fairy nodded and said:

"Cinder, you *shall* go to the ball."

And so, it was a week later, the evening of the ball arrived. The fairy had told Cinder that she would arrive promptly by six but the rat was getting impatient. She feared that her new friend would not be keeping her promise after all. She was so nervous, she almost gnawed off the end of her own tail. But fairies keep their promises – at least this one did – and she appeared in the alleyway outside the cellar window as the clock struck six.

"Are you ready, my dear?" she said sweetly, peeking her little face around the open window.

"Yes, I have been ready for this my whole life!" Cinder squealed, slipping out to join her.

"Then, let me begin showing you my gratitude."

And with a wave of her tiny wand, she began to mutter a spell. Magic dust exploded from its tip, falling all around Cinder like glittery flakes in a snow globe. Cinder began to scream. The transformation of a small rodent's body into that of a fully grown young adult was bound to be an unpleasant one. But I shall spare you the horror of hearing exactly what Cinder had to suffer through.

Besides, her joy at seeing herself in the reflection of a rain puddle made up for the agony. She was naked and as unaware and unashamed of it as Adam and Eve in Eden. In fact, Cinder was so proud of her new body, she was all ready to rush out of the alleyway and flaunt it to anyone who would look. The fairy, who had thus far been enjoying her happiness, decided to point out that such a thing might not be so wise.

"I must spin you a ball gown, my dear. Stand still a moment – "

And then with another wave of the wand, a swirl of glitter entwined around Cinder. When it scattered, she was swathed in a luxurious blue gown, the skirts falling to the ground in puffy tiers. The fairy thought it looked more like she was wearing a large birthday cake. But Cinder's delight convinced her that perhaps her sense of fashion was too razor sharp. She conjured a mask for the young female, having only just remembered it was a masquerade ball.

"The ball begins in an hour! But I don't know how far the castle is!" Cinder said.

"Worry not. I am prepared."

She certainly was. The fairy had been doing her grocery shopping earlier and had brought a baby pumpkin with the intent to enchant it. She took it out onto the street, peeked up and down to ensure no one was watching and tapped the pumpkin. It became the most marvellous carriage, sparkling and polished bright. A few of Cinder's rat friends had been watching all of this in awe from the cellar window and the fairy now asked them if they would help. They ran forward eagerly and she transformed two of them into liveried footmen. The other pair became magnificent white stallions, rearing at the head of the carriage. A passing cockroach was turned into a driver, without his permission, though he seemed to be pleased about the strange new development. His evening had been uneventful and he had not been looking forward to anything anyway.

"Hurry, hurry! You must set off!" the fairy called to Cinder, "but remember this, sweet Cinder, you must return before the stroke of midnight! That is when the magic will wear off and you will become a rat again! Do not forget!"

Cinder assured her she understood but the fairy was a little worried. She really did not look like she was in her right mind at all. It was too late. The cockroach driver shouted "Hey ho!" and off the carriage went.

The night was far more splendid than any fantasy Cinder had ever conjured in her mind. She walked into the room and it fell quiet. Only the barest of murmurs could be heard as she descended the stairs. Her heart felt like it would burst with delight.

They are all in awe of my beauty, she thought to herself.

She was indeed very beautiful. However, most people were gawping at the dress for it really did look like a birthday cake and was quite ridiculous. But Cinder did not notice the stifled giggles and shocked whispers. Her eyes searched for one face. The face she had only ever seen in her dreams.

The Prince was sitting grumpily at the far end of the hall, his mother and father on either side as his stern sentries. He had tried to get up more than a couple of times, yearning to return to his tower room. But his bodyguard's heavy hand pressed down on his shoulder whenever he did. The burly man was as much an obstacle as he was protection.

"See, who has arrived," his mother, the Queen, murmured to him. "Look at that girl yonder! How everyone marvels at her beauty! Go, dance with her! I do think she would make you a perfect wife!"

"They're marvelling at the fact she believed such a dress to be worthy of wearing in public," he grunted.

"Son, do as your mother says," the King hissed.

And since he was more afraid of his father, the Prince stood with a groan and straightened out his white jacket. Immediately, fans began to flutter and simpers echoed all around. Each young woman began to bat her lashes, hoping he was walking towards them. He parted them like the sea and made a beeline for the young lady in blue.

"Madame," he said, bowing low as he held out his hand.

Cinder turned such an alarming shade of red, the Prince feared she would faint. The last thing he wished to ruin his evening with was a fainting girl. But she gathered herself together and he was even more shocked to see how quickly the colour left her skin.

"Kind sir," she curtseyed, slipping her small hand into his.

'Kind sir? Why is she pretending she doesn't know who I am?' the Prince thought. He almost rolled his eyes but he could feel his father's stare burning into his head.

Cinder was in a realm of bliss which meant she could barely speak. The Prince however, tried to make polite conversation as he danced with her.

"What a remarkable dress," he commented, twirling her around and staring at the way her skirts billowed up. He tilted his head, frowned and added, "Goodness. And glass shoes. My, my, I wonder where you get your clothes made, Madame."

"A fairy made them," Cinder blurted out.

The Prince smiled, very slowly. "Of… course, my lady. What a talented fairy it must have been."

"She. It's a she."

"I see. Well, I must say, I'm never one to beat around the bush. Most of the time, that is. Sometimes, I like beating around - " he paused when he saw Cinder staring at him in confusion. He cleared his throat and pulled her closer with a fresh smile. "Never mind. What I mean to say, is that you look like you would make me a very good wife. If you promise not to bother me and leave me in peace, I will have all the dresses your heart desires made for you and you will live in the castle and one day become my Queen. Would you like that?"

Had Cinder been born human, she would perhaps have spied something awry in the Prince's proposal. But she was a rat and a gullible rat at that. She also forgot that she would soon return to *being* a rat. Exhilaration took over and she almost screamed "Yes!" But at the last minute, she lowered her voice and whispered her answer, nodding emphatically to back it up.

The Prince nodded with a bored sigh and said, "Well, so it shall be. Stay behind after the ball and – "

The clock began to strike the hour.

Cinder jumped in fright. By the Goddess! She had forgotten the time! She ripped herself from the Prince's arms – quite literally, for her sleeve had caught on his gold sleeve buttons and had ripped – before turning on her heel and rushing towards the exit. The Prince stood there in complete shock. He could not comprehend what had just happened. Rather than call the guards to chase her, he began to chase after her himself. What a night this was turning out to be.

"Madame! Madame, wait!" he called after her.

He could see the blue of her dress in the distance, glowing in the moonlight. He sped up but she really was quite a good runner.

"You didn't even tell me your name!"

Cinder was no longer listening. She tripped, losing a single glass shoe on her way to where the carriage had been. But just as she got there, she saw a spark of glitter fade and the carriage was a pumpkin once more. Her rat friends saw her and squeaked, alerting her to where they were.

She cried out, falling to her knees as the transformation began to happen. It was quicker this time and before she knew it, she was being suffocated by the plentiful folds of her dress. With the help of her friends and the abnormally large cockroach, she escaped it and had enough presence of mind to drag it along with her. Between them, they carried the dress and the remaining glass shoe with them, scurrying as fast as they could, back to their cellar under the merchant's house.

Behind them, the Prince picked up the glass shoe and stared at in silence.

"I suppose I'll have to marry that irritatingly chatty princess my mother suggested last week. What a shame."

He flung the shoe at a nearby statue. It shattered into a thousand iridescent pieces. He stood still for a moment, pondering. Then, he turned and walked back up towards the castle, thinking he would never see the strange girl in blue again.

No, the story does not end here.

Cinder being Cinder, had become quite addicted to her first and only experience of being a human girl. As the days wore on, she just could not become accustomed to living life as a rat once more. She stopped eating, she couldn't sleep and she didn't talk or smile. The only rats who knew the reason behind her depression were the ones who had been turned into her footmen and the horses that pulled her carriage. They were kind hearted friends and though she treated them quite rudely sometimes, they decided they had to find the fairy again and entreat her to help Cinder.

But she was not easy to find.

In fact, had she not decided to visit Cinder herself a week later, they would never have found her. The fairy was quite distressed to see the state of her friend and she anxiously asked if something had gone wrong or if her magic had failed.

"N-no, nothing like that," Cinder stuttered, sniffing and wiping her nose with her tail. "I just – oh, I just – I wish I could be human forever! The Prince he proposed to me! But before I could accept in front of everyone, the clock struck midnight and I had to return! Now he will marry someone else and he would have married me! I would have been *Queen*!"

And she lapsed into a fresh fit of sobs.

No matter how the fairy tried to console her, Cinder would not be comforted. It broke the fairy's heart to see her friend in such a state. Cinder was not lying. Just today, it had been announced throughout the kingdom that the Prince would be marrying a princess from a neighbouring land. The wedding was to be held next month.

As she sat there, stroking Cinder's back, a very terrible idea crept into the fairy's mind.

"I think there might be a way to make the spell permanent," she whispered.

She was almost hoping Cinder would not hear. But she had a rat's sense of hearing and it was very sharp. Her head swivelled around and she stared at the fairy, her large black eyes brimming with unshed tears.

"Please tell me," she begged.

The fairy decided there was nothing for it.

"It requires a life for a life. It is the only way to remain human forever. For you to be his bride, you must kill the princess on their wedding night and climb into bed with the Prince. Once the clock strikes midnight, you will assume her form and she will transform into a rat - though very much a dead rat, I'm afraid. That is the only way I know."

Cinder tensed up. Murder? Was she capable of it? Her heart failed her.

But then, she remembered the eyes on her, the silkiness of her dress and the warmth of the Prince's breath on her ear as he whispered into it.

Conscience be damned. Perhaps the princess is a bad person and I would be doing everyone a service.

Rather weak reasoning but love is not known for its astute rationality.

Cinder agreed and asked the fairy how such a thing would come about. The fairy told her that she would make her a potion for Cinder to drink. It was not poisonous for rats but it was deadly for humans. All Cinder would have to do upon reaching the Prince's bedroom, was relieve herself in the princess's drink until her bladder was empty. It would take a few hours to take full effect and by the time it did, the princess would be dead in her bed.

It took the fairy exactly a month to concoct the potion, a riveting coincidence by all accounts. Cinder spent the next four weeks saying her goodbyes to her family and promising that she would rescue them when she was the princess and they would live the rest of their days in luxury. She had quite forgotten that rats did not live very long.

Thus, a month passed and the Prince's wedding drew near.

The day arrived and Cinder's friend brought the tiny vial of potion she had so painstakingly prepared. She repeated her instructions and sternly admonished Cinder for forgetting to heed her words the last time. Cinder was very much sober now – murder was no joking matter – and she assured the fairy she understood.

She bid a tearful farewell to each and every member of the rat community. The last goodbye was reserved for her fairy friend.

"You must come and visit me soon," Cinder wept, as she hugged her, "I would love for you to be the fairy godmother of my future children."

The fairy said she would love that and after another hug, waved her off. Cinder looked back at the alleyway where the small group of rats and the fairy stood together. She waved her tail one last time, a fat tear rolling down from her eye, before scurrying across the pavement. The vial was in her mouth and she was not to drink from it until she had reached the castle.

Cinder's heart beat with excitement. This was going to be the start of her new life! This was –

"Well, hello there."

Cinder had only just turned the corner of the street before a slender, gnarly hand reached down and scooped her up.

It was a tall, skinny man, dressed from head to toe in colourful jester's attire. He had a hooked nose, a pointy chin and beady eyes that sparkled with mischief. In one hand, he twirled a flute. He seemed very pleased to see Cinder and did not appear to understand her frantic squeaking at all.

"You're going to come in very handy on my next trade stop," he murmured, stroking a thumb over her head.

He slipped her inside a wicker cage and slammed the lid closed. With a merry whistle, he kicked his heels together and danced down the street. Once he was beyond the city walls, it took him only minutes to find the yellow brick road and embark upon it. As he walked, he sang a little tune:

"Hey ho, hey ho, off to Hamlin we go!"

Golden Eyes

Part III

Thirteen days and thirteen nights,

Golden Eyes waited for the

Goblin King to return.

efore she left his hut, she had stolen his flute. She played it, on and on, until her throat was parched. She knew not why she cried for him. He was a trickster, a scoundrel, a deceitful teller of falsehoods! He had hidden the passing of time from her by strange manners of enchantment. He confounded her. And now, she had no family, she had no life, she had no home

At first, she called to him out of anger. So determined was she that she would find some way to get her revenge, she thought of nothing else. Red, red, scarlet red was all she saw. Her cloak was muddied, her shoes were stained. Their red could barely be seen. The red before her eyes was the only red left.

Her anger wore out and there was nothing but an aching hollow in her stomach.

Loneliness. And fear – fear that he would never return. He had forsaken her. She was to die in this forest, wretched and alone.

Golden Eyes survived on berries and the water from babbling brooks. Woodland creatures bounded here and there but she did not know how to hunt and her taste for meat had vanished a long time ago. If only their harmless trills, squeaks and howls were all that she heard. For in the distance, always far enough to keep her from bounding like a frightened March hare, were the haunting sounds of creatures as old as the forest itself. They were not animals and neither were they human. They sounded like nothing she had heard before.

Golden Eyes teetered on the edge of madness, though sometimes, she felt she had already fallen over it.

And it was there, on the brink, that she met her grandmother.

A dream? Surely, it must be so. Her grandmother should have been long dead. And yet as she walked closer, she saw that her grandmother was wearing her patchwork dress, in tatters at the hem, and that her grey hair was braided under her cap. She had her cauldron before her, stirring it slowly. The leathery tan skin of her face stretched into a little smile and she reached for Golden Eyes.

"Grandmama..." the young girl croaked. "Grandmama, is it really you? Help me, I am ruined..."

Her grandmother did not answer.

The air grew stale, carrying with it the stench of death. Golden Eyes retched, but there was nothing in her stomach to heave up. When her grandmother touched her head, the smell intensified.

"Grandmama, am I dying?" she cried helplessly. "Why is this happening to me? I am sorry! So, so sorry for not heeding your warnings!"

Her grandmother cackled. "Child, my warnings were meant to be ignored. For had you heeded them, the Erl King would not have received his due payment. It was a yearly matter you know. Many a young thing has been delivered into his clutches so that he may leave the rest of us in peace. Everyone has their price to pay. Your mother paid dearly for hers and slept a hundred years. But now, she is a Queen and her children will rule a kingdom. Wait patiently, for you may still get the reward for your price..."

Golden Eyes reached up a hand to her but the old woman came apart, her body turning into dust that swirled once in the churning air and then vanished. Nothing made sense to the golden-eyed waif. Nothing at all. She heard and saw little, except for her grandmother's cackling in her ears and the angry bubbling of her cauldron. How she loved to stir that cauldron…it was so very like…the one he had…

Golden Eyes drifted into a dreamless sleep.

When she awoke, she found her cheek resting on sun baked loam. With a start, she lifted herself from the floor, staring around her in wonder. There, by the hearth he sat, stirring his cauldron and singing ancient hymns under his breath. His hair fell like a curtain of snow, hiding his face but there was a lightness to his tone and from time to time, he snickered under his breath.

"Do you think leaving me to fend for myself for thirteen days and thirteen nights qualifies as some form of amusement?" Golden Eyes spat.

She marched over to him, meaning to snatch a handful of his hair and hurt him, just like he had hurt her. But his hand stopped her in time, catching her around the waist and causing her to tumble into his lap.

"Be not ill-tempered, child, for it was you who threw the first stone," he said, complacent and calm.

"You disappeared!"

"You ran away."

"You knew I had nowhere to run too! Yet you frightened me, for you are a miscreant and I should never have run into your kingdom in the first place!"

"And yet you did."

He released her and she fell to the floor, throwing off her scarlet cloak and shoes. Golden Eyes did not move, for she could see what was in the cauldron and it made her stomach rumble. The Goblin King watched her as he stirred, the hunger in her eyes only amusing him further. A bubble popped in the soup and Golden Eyes remembered.

"I saw my grandmother in the woods," she said.

The Goblin King snickered. "I am sure you did. She is a witch. Witches thrive in these woods."

"Is she dead?"

"I know not."

"Did she promise me to you?"

"Did you ask her?"

"Why must you answer my questions with irritating questions of your own?"

"Why must you ask such aimless questions?"

"They are not aimless! I wish to know! She said my mother ran away but now she tells me my mother is a queen!"

"She is. A queen with a penchant for poisoned apples and mirrors." And then he laughed, a roaring sound.

"That must mean my grandmother is as evil as you are," Golden Eyes said.

The resignation in her voice forced him to turn his head towards her.

"Evil is a matter of personal perspective."

And he would say no more.

Golden Eyes complied, asking no questions. She enjoyed the food he had cooked and she enjoyed the passion of his body. She had missed both dearly. But for the first time in many moons, as the Goblin King thrust her into the numbing darkness she craved, the sounds of their crying went with her.

The mournful wails of his caged, feathered prisoners followed her into the bottomless abyss.

Once he has you, he keeps you.
He destroys you,
he skins you,
he leaves you out to dry.
The Goblin King is something worse,
much worse than the devils of old.

Snow White

*O*nce upon an occasion, a young King sat on the window sill of his bedroom, watching the first snowfall.

It had been a terrible year for the kingdom. They had lost a war and forfeited the most valuable part of their empire. Last year had not been any good either. The King's parents had died in a freak accident involving a pair of mad horses. The year prior and the King – who had then been a Prince – had mistakenly brought the wrong girl from the neighbouring kingdom, thinking she was the princess, when in fact, she was just a lowly maid. He had married her whilst she was trapped in the hold of a sleeping curse. Still asleep, she had birthed him a son who had died a year later.

All in all, the last three years had been troublesome for the young King.

The first snowfall was a blanket of healing, layering over the wounds his land had suffered and kissing them better. It was a blank sheet of nothing. A new start.

"Come. Look how the snow falls," he called to his wife.

The Queen cowered in a corner, grabbing her shuddering knees to her chest. Her lip was cut, her eye was bruised and she had various injuries all over her body. Her husband had made a habit of violently painting her body with the evidence of his growing insanity. She feared he would one day break all the bones in her body and no one would be any the wiser. The kingdom had not batted an eye when he married her whilst she was asleep. They had not cared how insidious it was that she had birthed him a son whilst dead to the world. The kingdom was not her friend. She had no friends.

But upon his gentle command, she forced her worn body into motion. At first, she crawled, not able to stand. Her trembling fingers found the bed posts and she heaved herself up, sealing in whimpers behind chapped lips. It took her six more limping steps before she fell onto the window seat behind him. Her once luscious, golden locks were tangled and her skin was a harsh white.

"It is beautiful, my love," she whispered, her eyes empty as they took in the falling snow.

"I do agree," he said, "in fact, it brings to mind an impromptu wish."

"What is that, my love?"

"I wish to have another child."

The King was so enraptured by this new desire he failed to notice his wife recoil at his words. He continued, blissfully unaware.

"And he will be the most beautiful in the land. He will bring a new age to our beloved kingdom and he will be my heir. I wish that he would have hair as black as unsullied ebony, skin as pure and fresh as the whitest snow and lips…"

He turned his head to notice the red drops of scarlet on the snow drenched sill. The Queen had coughed mildly, causing the cut in her lip to ooze fresh blood. The King smiled.

"And lips as red as blood, my dear."

She smiled, her lips straining and bleeding harder. "Of course, Your Majesty. You deserve to have all your wishes granted."

There was an amicable silence in which they gazed at one another. Then –

"Well, get on the bed and spread your legs, kitchen wench. My son won't just materialise out of thin air."

Kitchen wench. Cruelty on top of cruelty. It never ended. He never failed to remind her that her status in life was but an unlucky mistake. A mistake on his part after being bewitched by what he called her 'evil beauty'. She had never bothered to inform him that her position had been that of a handmaiden and she had never even seen the kitchens of the castle she had lived in.

But she was well used to taking orders, be it from her witch mother in the past, or her husband in the present. The Queen did her duty now also, allowing the King to put his wish into effect.

And outside, the snow continued to fall.

The Queen's pregnancy lasted all of ten months. One month too long. In that last month, she was afraid the King would beat the baby out of her belly in his impatience. She did not think she would be able to bear it if something happened to her second child.

To that effect, she had not spent ten months in solitary confinement in vain.

The Queen may not have been born royal. But she had a rather interesting genealogy. Coming from a long line of witches, her mother had been the most powerful sorceress in the land. It was upon her behest that the Queen had saved a single needle when she had served the princess of the neighbouring land. All the needles in the land had been destroyed by the princess's concerned parents save for the one the maid had been given by her conniving witch mother. What the witch had failed to tell her was that her life was expendable. In fact, pricking her finger would make all in the princess's vicinity fall asleep, not just her alone.

This betrayal by her mother was the sole reason the Queen had not searched her out upon waking up. She had no use for a woman who had no use for her. So, she bore the pain of marriage to a man she did not love and resigned herself to a life in quarantine.

But there was a limit to anyone's patience.

Ten months the Queen attempted to learn the magic her mother had been so skilled at. After all, she had the blood of witches in her veins. She was sure she could concoct a potion as potent as any her mother might conjure.

The birth of her second child fell on the first day of autumn. It took hours and hours before a beautiful little girl was born. Upon taking the child to her bosom, the Queen was overwhelmed with joy. She could not remember ever feeling such happiness as she gazed upon the baby's dear little face.

"Lips as red as blood, skin as white as snow and hair as black as ebony…if only queenly wishes would come true with such auspiciousness," she sighed to herself.

Alas, when the King heard the child was a girl, he went mad with rage and refused to see her. Instead, he gathered a hunting party and went out to the forest to hunt wild boar. He shouted a curse towards the Queen's tower window before riding out of the courtyard. Though the servants hurried to close the windows, she heard it and her face blanched. And she knew what she had to do.

It was time.

The King returned a week later, having sated himself with wine, wild boar and whores aplenty. He was in a far merrier mood and wished to see his wife that night. There was no mention of the child. The Queen was still in no condition to serve her husband's lewd desires but she knew he did not take no for an answer. So, she put on her finest clothes and had the maids comb and tease her golden hair, pinning it with a tiara.

She gazed at herself in the mirror and smiled. She was beautiful once more. Every soul she passed on her way to the King's chambers made no secret of staring. It was as if a heavenly angel herself had alighted upon the earth and walked in their midst. She may have been born a maid but she possessed an angelic beauty and regal bearing that very few could boast of.

Before she entered her husband's chambers, she snapped her fingers and turned to one of her maids. The young girl scurried forward with a basket filled with sweetmeats, covered by a silken cloth. They were all the King's favourites and she had had them specially made.

He was overjoyed to see her, twirling her around and laughing jovially. In fact, he was in such a good mood, she thought to mention their child. But she held her tongue. There was no need.

"My love, you must be hungry. Before we go to bed, I would that you taste some of the gifts I bear you," she said, sweetly caressing his bearded cheek.

Something dark flickered in the King's eyes and he sneered. "A Queen who gives gifts in the form of petty confectionery. My, my, whenever I am dazzled by your beauty, I am quickly reminded of what low status you are."

"Not all gifts made of love require pearls and jewels to be embedded in them," she said gently.

And for once, her husband did not argue.

She uncovered the basket and bade him sit. It was brimming with sweets, but in its centre, sat a rosy red apple. The King was riveted.

"What a marvellous fruit. Pray tell where you picked it," he murmured.

The Queen smirked and lifted the succulent, scarlet apple, cradling it between her snowy white fingers.

"The Tree of Knowledge. I journeyed far in your name, so that you may taste the sweet poison of my love for you," she said.

"Poison, is it?" he guffawed, snatching it from her.

"Yes. Poison," she smiled.

"Then, let me taste this poison of yours. Surely, it cannot be as bitter as that which you hold between your legs," he sneered.

And he took a huge bite. The fruit burst, its juices dribbling from the corners of his mouth and staining his beard. But the stain was red, as if it were a strawberry, not an apple. He chewed loudly, smacking his lips and turning the apple from side to side.

"I do say, this is the strangest fruit I have ever eaten," he mused.

Then, he turned a deep shade of puce and keeled over, dead.

"I told you it was poison, my love. Ever the violent, impetuous fool," the Queen said.

And so, it was that the King of the land died of a most terrible and unknown malady. As custom dictated, his only living heir, Snow White, became the next monarch of the kingdom. After a week's mourning and funeral rites, the news was announced and the land sank into despair. How was a baby girl going to rule them? They were doomed to the bitter fate of civil war!

Their fears were unwarranted.

The Queen took over as Regent, ruling on behalf of her only child. She surprised everyone with her adeptness at political craft and it was not long before she had smoothed out the many tangled policies her husband had laid in place. She had finally found her calling and she took to it like a moth to a flame.

However, her husband left his sullied mark upon her.

The Queen always knew the dead King had remained married to her because of her exquisite beauty. She had been often termed "the fairest in all the land" and he had taken every opportunity to remind her that her beauty was the only reason for her salvation. Without him to tell her this now, the demons of her mind began to play their games.

The Queen began to grow afraid her beauty was wearing out with every passing year. She was always afraid there would one day be someone more beautiful than she. And that, she could not bear.

Once again, she reached for her old magic books and began to search up all the spells she could find to preserve her looks. But none was as effective as a curse she found and that, was the most loathsome of them all.

It required the caster to bathe in the blood of a young virgin at every full moon.

The Queen was horrified and put away her books, swearing to never look inside them again.

The years wore on and Snow White grew up, becoming as beautiful as her dear mother and just as intelligent. But there was something odd about her. Her nursemaids noticed it first. But they dared not mention it to the Queen for fear she would be furious and accuse them of insinuating something was not quite right with the little princess. For they had come to realise Snow White was happiest when she was the cause of physical pain for other living beings.

She had never laughed brighter than when she kicked her pet cat off the window sill of the highest tower. The poor little thing broke every bone in its body and survived for only a few minutes after. She collected the feathers of birds she had plucked raw, turning them into dream-catchers that she hung up all over her room.

But she particularly enjoyed tormenting her maids. She would create all sorts of elaborate booby traps and contraptions, designed to have her victim screaming in pain. It was not long before her retinue of maids was being changed weekly. No one could handle the child for long and some whispered that she was the child of the Erl King himself. She must be! Both her parents were golden haired and she had been born with jet black locks. There had to be some maleficent blood in her veins.

But her servants managed to keep her mother unaware of Snow White's growing sadism.

On Snow White's fifteenth birthday, the Queen threw a magnificent ball, inviting royals and officials from all the other kingdoms. Everyone marvelled at what a lovely girl the princess had become. She dazzled all eyes in her pearly white gown, diamonds sparkling in her ebony curls and lips stained an inviting shade of red. All agreed that a prettier girl could not be found far and wide.

The Queen revelled in this admiration of her daughter's beauty. Snow White was her flesh and blood after all and shared her mother's charms. But an uneasy feeling crept up on her as the night wore on. Not a single person had complimented her on how stunning *she* looked tonight. Her gown was gold, a tad lighter than her hair, flowing down her slender body in liquid swirls. Her eyes were sparkling pools of darkness in a face as fair as the sun. Had her daughter not been the centre of attention, the Queen would still have commanded all hearts in the room. But with Snow White present, it was impossible.

My looks are fading.

The thought echoed in her mind, refusing to leave her be even when she went to bed later that night. Something had changed. She could swear there were faint wrinkles around her eyes and just last week, she had plucked a silver thread amongst all the gold growing from her scalp. She looked young but she felt old inside and it was a feeling unlike any other.

Once more, the Queen decided her witch's blood would serve her well.

This time, she did not shiver upon studying that loathsome curse she had rejected years ago. Instead, she pored over it, deciding the best way to fulfil its nefarious ends.

And it was so, that when the tenth cat Snow White was gifted, fell onto the Queen's balcony, she received the means to her end. The maids were going quite out of their minds once they found the princess on the roof. They chastised her for still maintaining such bad behaviour even after growing into a young woman. The Queen heard them chiding the girl, her eyes fixed on the mangled animal at her feet.

The falling snow was already covering it, a funeral shroud of white.

Still, she was not convinced. It was not until a handmaiden of the princess's brought her Snow White's journal, trembling and in fear of her life, that the Queen understood her daughter's innate inclinations. Over the span of ten pages, Snow White had meticulously drawn out diagrams describing how she intended to "help" the poor dwarf jesters at court and give them a normal height. Her plan involved sewing them together in pairs, cutting off limbs, joining and then reattaching them to resemble longer, human arms. Nowhere in her plans was there any mention of keeping them alive. She just wished to see them taller.

The Queen realised it was a monster she and the King had created. Out of hatred and fear, sprang violence. Snow White was her only child but the Queen was no fool. She saw her for what she was.

It would be better that I live forever and rule this land, than let it fall into her hands.

For a year, Snow White's mother learned her daughter's ways. She studied her temperament, her habits, her conversation. Meanwhile, she had a chamber constructed beside her bedroom, hidden by a secret door set into the north facing wall. She commissioned the construction of a magnificent mirror, bordered with a heavy silver frame and fitted onto the wall. But this was no ordinary mirror.

It opened like a small door, the front lifting away to reveal another mirror underneath. The reflective surface of this second mirror faced into the secret chamber. It became a window for the Queen to see into the room, yet anyone inside would only see their face reflected back to them, none the wiser that they were being watched.

And on her sixteenth birthday, this chamber was Snow White's gift.

The Queen did not have to explain. Her daughter's eyes lit up when she saw the array of tools on the wall, an altar with straps attached to the middle, chains hanging from the ceiling and torches - so many torches - fitted into iron brackets. It was a torture chamber. There was no other description for it.

"Mother! Am I to carry out my experiments here? Oh, you *are* kind! How did you know this was what I wanted?" Snow

White exclaimed, clapping her hands together in glee.

"In return for this room, my love, you must promise to heed a few of your mother's wishes. For I created this room purely for the sake of my daughter's happiness," the Queen answered.

"Of course, mother, but – but Nanny told me I mustn't hurt living creatures. She said that the kingdom would revolt against a future Queen who hurts others," Snow White said slowly.

A shadow was cast over the Queen's face. She took Snow White by the shoulders and tilted her chin up with a finger.

"Your Nanny is a hypocrite and a fool," she said. "When your father, the King, was still alive, she was my chambermaid. She stood by and she listened as he tortured me every night. She would listen to my screams and she would pretend she did not see my bruises and my cuts. She had no qualms in becoming one of his many whores and actively tried to give him the son he so desired. She was his favourite mistress, though she remained barren. And since she did not allow it, no other servant dared give me the human kindness I had starved for since the day I was born. It took me far too long to grow up and realise kindness is a lie. No good deed goes unpunished, as they say. Thus, I decided I would be the punisher of those who would dare to commit good deeds and bolster their fragile sensibilities by convincing themselves they are worthy of the Goddess who made them. And you, my love…"

The Queen's eyes brimmed with tears of emotion as she took Snow White's face into her hands.

"You will be the judge, jury and executioner I was loathe to be for so long. You will not repeat my mistakes. You will be the fear of all who dare to underestimate you. And look, I have prepared another gift for you. This chamber does not come empty."

Two spots of red appeared in Snow White's pale cheeks at these words. She became feverish with excitement as the Queen clapped her hands briskly. Two bulky guards dragged in a bound and gagged woman. It was Snow White's Nanny.

When the Queen returned to her room, she tested out the mirror. It worked beautifully. She could see everything her daughter did inside the room and Snow White did everything for the mirror, almost as if she was orchestrating a performance. It appeared she was quite fond of her own reflection. *So very*

like her father in that respect, the Queen
thought.

She fiddled with her wedding ring as she
watched the life drain out of her old enemy. For
so long, she had pretended to forgive the
Nanny, letting her think she was safe from
retribution. But she had simply been waiting
for the right punishment. And it was finally
here. She almost wished she could hear her
screams; she looked as if she were in the
utmost pain. But once Snow White began to
flay her, it became too much for even the
Queen to watch and she covered up the smaller
mirror once again.

Three years passed in which Snow White
was groomed by her mother to become a
dutiful huntress and butcher. The wayward
princess developed a habit of dressing as a
commoner and stalking the city at night,
keeping an eye out for potential victims. Her
mother expressed a preference for young,
virginal girls and Snow White did not question
her. She just wanted one thing.

And so, it was that the Queen looked
younger and more beautiful every year. Many
marvelled at this splendid phenomenon. A few
whispered of it being the result of some sinister
black magic, but those were few and far
between. The ones who were particularly vocal

about it, found themselves becoming acquainted with the sharp edge of Snow White's blade.

Over the years, the people of the land began to marry off their daughters immediately after their first blood, to save them from being stolen away. No one knew quite where they were taken but the Queen's vigour and beauty was telling enough. And people loved to speculate. But she was unchallenged and her reign continued in glory.

Until one day, the royal huntress encountered a girl she would not have had the heart to kill, even if she could.

There was nothing particularly remarkable about this particular personage. She had mousey brown hair, a sweet smile and blue eyes the colour of a cloudless sky. And she was lame.

Snow White approached her in the woods as she picked berries for a pie she was going to be baking for the children of the neighbourhood later. Upon seeing another young woman, as beautiful and as dainty as Snow White, the girl did not find any reason to be alarmed. She shared with the princess that her name was Cornflower and upon being asked, told her of how she had come to need her crutches.

"I was lame since birth. The doctor took one look at my curved spine and said I would never walk without aid again. And so, I had to find support elsewhere."

"Such an unfortunate fate," Snow White murmured.

"Not at all. The Goddess gives and takes in Her own wisdom," Cornflower replied cheerfully. "For I was the only child in the town that I grew up in. All the adults doted upon me and I never wanted for love or for clothes and food or drink. I was an orphan soon after birth but I was loved and cared for. A blessing others like me do not often experience."

Snow White laughed brightly. "The only child in the town? Goodness! How could that be? What a remarkable happening that the Goddess should curse an entire town with infertility and provide them with an orphan child to dote upon!"

At this moment, Cornflower noticed something was rather queer about Snow White's mannerisms. She did not appear to carry about her the social decorum that young ladies her age were trained to have. She was too blunt in speech and the delicateness of her features was absent in her behaviour. But there was something endearing about her ignorance.

"They were not infertile – and other children were born later. But when I was very young, about six or seven I would say, the town was plagued by an infestation of rats. We could not be rid of them until the day a tall, thin man dressed in all the colours under the sun, offered to do the job. And he did, using a flute he always carried at his belt. It was quite marvellous watching him lead away the hordes of vermin, all piling on top of one another like waves in a dark, murky river. But alas, the townspeople refused to pay him when he returned to ask for the reward they had offered. As revenge, he played an altogether different tune on his pipe and he took all the children with him – "

Cornflower stopped, impeded from continuing by a lump in her throat. Her eyes filled with tears and she seemed to be seeing something very far away, something Snow White could not. She stood in silence, until she had blinked away her tears and her voice became steady once more.

"I still remember the tune he played," she murmured, wiping her tears off one of the berries in her basket. "It was the most beautiful sound I had ever heard. I dream of it sometimes, that soaring, glorious melody, promising that I would get everything I had ever wanted if I followed it. All the little children danced and followed him, but I – I could not. For I was a lame, little girl and my crutches could not carry me fast enough. The last child turned the corner of the road and the sound of the flute disappeared and I just sat down and I – well, I cried my heart out. I remained there in the hopes that he would return for me but he never did. The baker found me and carried me back to the town where everyone was in the streets, wailing and screaming for their lost children."

Cornflower took a deep, trembling breath, wiping her eyes and giving a brave smile.

"Where did he take the children?" Snow White asked curiously, for her mind was always taken in by the strange and unnatural and this was a mystery she was fascinated by.

"I do not know. The priestess said that he was a demon and he had taken the children somewhere very bad."

"What a strange thing to tell a child."

"The priestesses of the Goddess are not known for their softness, I suppose. But I did not believe her. I am sure he took them to heaven. Or somewhere very much like heaven. And I regret to this day that I did not leave with him. It was the only time I cursed myself for being lame."

Snow White stared at her in silence. Then, her blood red lips wavered, slowly curving up. It was as if she was learning to smile for the first time and the muscles in her face refused to cooperate for a moment. In fact, Cornflower felt quite concerned, the harder she saw Snow White fight against herself. But finally, she had on a semblance of what was a sweet, kind smile and she reached out to pat Cornflower's shoulder.

"If you had gone with him, I would never have met you. And that would be quite awful," Snow White said.

Cornflower laughed, a shaky sound. But she smiled, and she did a far better job of it than the princess as she laid her hand over Snow White's pale one.

"You are very sweet," she said.

"What was the name of the town you grew up in? Perhaps I may make enquiries after this strange man and hunt him down."

"Hamlin. Dare I ask how you will do such a thing?" Cornflower asked curiously.

Snow White smirked, a sinister expression. "I have many resources at my beck and call. Worry not, Lady Cornflower. One day

I will bring this piper before you and have him tell you if it really was heaven where he took the children of Hamlin."

There was more than confusion in Cornflower's heart as she bid goodbye to Snow White that afternoon. It was a feeling that quite frightened her at first before she realised it was making her feel warm. It was not *quite* like it, but was very close to the emotion she had experienced upon hearing the Piper's song in Hamlin.

Upon her return to the castle that evening, Snow White informed her mother the Queen that she had not managed to find a single victim. Her mother was perturbed but not desperate for she had a supply of blood that she could still use. However, Snow White had never returned empty handed after a hunt. For this reason alone, the Queen called one of her guards to ask of him the reason behind today's lack of results.

This guard had followed Snow White discretely on each of her hunts, for the princess liked to go alone. The Queen trusted in her daughter's cold, calculated ability but she was the only living heir to the throne. Her mother was worried for her safety and she sent her own henchman to make sure Snow White remained out of trouble.

And so it was, that the Queen learned about Snow White's meeting with Cornflower.

She was livid.

The very next morning, she ordered Snow White to her chambers and demanded that Cornflower's blood be drained from her body to become the contents of her next bath. The princess did not argue. It frightened her mother to see her daughter so changed. Snow White's fiery temper failed to flare as strongly as it usually did.

Instead, she knelt before her mother, her head bowed.

"What is the meaning of this? Stand! Queens do not kneel!" her mother bellowed.

"I am no Queen, mother. You are Queen," was Snow White's placid remark. "I will never be Queen, because you will never die. You will always bathe in the blood of young virgins and will become immortal."

Rage twisted the Queen's beautiful features, making her look wretched and ugly as the sun dipped behind the clouds outside the window. But then, her expression cleared and the sunlight returned. She reached down and helped her daughter stand, her eyes filled with love.

"You wish to be Queen, is that it?" she asked. "I will abdicate in your honour, my darling. You will rule the kingdom that is your birth right. This I promise you."

"I do not wish to rule, mother," Snow White said. "I will bring you all the blood you need, but I will not bring you Cornflower's."

And no matter how her mother reasoned with her, she would not give in. The Queen could not have that.

"You will obey me! Cornflower's lifeless, bloodless body will be stretched out in the mirror chamber tomorrow night or I will have her hanged, drawn and quartered like the whore that she is!"

Snow White blanched. "How did you know that she is – how did you know?"

The Queen said nothing, realising her mistake. Cornflower's blood was of no use to her. The girl was not a virgin. But the Queen had always been vengeful and that had not changed.

But her daughter was not stupid. It was Snow White's turn to shake with rage.

"You had her followed?" she shouted. "How could you? After the loyalty I showed you!"

"And yet your loyalty was for naught," the Queen sneered. "I was right to have my man follow both of you. You were going to lie to me? Over a common whore off the streets of the city? Your father would be ashamed of you!"

"You killed my father so I would not know, would I?"

"Snow White, enough!" the Queen roared. "Tomorrow night, I will have the whore brought to the mirror chamber and I will have her tortured before you! You will learn what it is to be obedient once more, I promise you that!"

As soon as she was dismissed, Snow White wasted no time in disguising herself and rushing from the castle. She had many guards who were loyal to her and all of them would rather cut out their own tongues than betray her to the Queen.

The princess found Cornflower at the end of a street in the slums, near where she lived. She was trying to sell her wares for the night.

"Come with me! Hurry!" Snow White hissed, grabbing her elbow and rushing her away.

"Stop! You mustn't! I will be whipped if I do not bring in at least ten gold coins tonight!"

Cornflower panicked, struggling to keep up on her crutches, "the Madame will have my head!"

"I will have hers!" Snow White exclaimed, halting abruptly. She lowered her hood, revealing the coronet on her black hair. Two men stepped from the shadows behind her, dressed in the garb of the royal guard and the realisation struck Cornflower like a ton of bricks.

With a gasp, she fell to her knees, lowering her head in reverence.

"We do not have time!" the princess said, pulling her back to her feet with impatience. "My mother the Queen wishes to have you executed tomorrow and I am here to save you!"

She did not explain the wherefores of the matter and commanded one of her men to provide Cornflower with a seat on his horse. They rode back to the castle at high speed and were inside before the changing of the guard.

Cornflower spent a terrifying night and half a day locked away in the princess's bedchamber. She thought it was all just an awful dream and she would wake at any minute. Why would the Queen wish to execute her? There were many other women like her, and men too, making their money in the darkness of night. Why should she alone warrant such a cruel end?

Questions whirled in her mind and they got no reprieve for Snow White did not make an appearance until night fell once more.

And when she arrived, she looked magnificent.

Now Cornflower saw her for the royalty she was. And seeing how her snowy skin glowed, her hair gleamed and her eyes sparkled, she thought herself foolish for not guessing upon first seeing Snow White. She did not even need the crown she wore or the shimmering dress. She was a princess by blood.

"Your Highness, I – " she began to say, but Snow White cut her off.

"You will call me Snow White," she said sternly. Then after some hesitation, she said, "I-I would quite like it if you called me that."

"Yes, Your – Snow White," Cornflower murmured, a tentative smile gracing her lips. "But the Queen, your mother – "

"You are safe," the princess beamed. She held out her hand, laden with rings and bracelets, and Cornflower took it. "Come with me, dear. I have something for you."

Snow White took her up to the Queen's bedchambers. Had Cornflower known where she was, she would have fainted from terror. But she did not. To her, they were just another set of rooms, as marvellous as any other in the castle. The mirror delighted her. When Snow White pulled it back, the chamber beyond could be seen. But it looked to be an altogether different room now. There were no tools hanging from the walls, the chains were gone and it was furnished to look quite cosy, complete with a fire flickering in the grate. And at its centre, was a bath filled with –

"My goodness, what is that?" Cornflower murmured.

Snow White grinned. "That is my gift for you. Come."

She led the young woman inside and Cornflower recoiled at the coppery scent. She knew what it was now.

"Do not be alarmed!" Snow White said quickly.

"It is blood – "

"It is! But it's the blood of a very special creature! One of the last to exist in this world. A unicorn. It will heal you, my love. I swear it."

Cornflower's limbs trembled. Fear? Excitement? She did not know. This day had been entirely too much. But seeing Snow White's kind smile, she could not help but let her heart be soothed. Shyly, she began to take off her dress, allowing the princess to help her. The soaring emotion returned when Snow White's soft hand touched her skin and Cornflower's blue eyes glittered.

She sank into the bath, a weak sigh leaving her lips. Her eyes closed and she rested her head on the edge, falling into a slumber. Snow White sat down beside the marble tub and watched her, mesmerised by the sight.

Cornflower slept in the bath all night.

And in the morning, when she awoke and looked around for her crutches, she discovered that she was moving nimbly. Her back was no longer aching as it always did after a long rest. She could not speak, she could not make a sound, she was so overcome. Beside her, Snow White was asleep in her chair.

And Cornflower cried tears of pure joy.

She reached out and kissed the princess's ruby lips. Slowly, Snow White's eyelashes fluttered open and the first things she saw were Cornflower's bright blue eyes shining with happiness. Not a word was exchanged for Snow White to understand that her spell had worked. They just kissed and cried and embraced, their heartbeats synchronised into a pounding crescendo of delight.

It was announced to the horrified people of the land that the Queen Mother had been a witch who had used her own subjects to lengthen her life by unnatural means. Upon discovering her atrocities, Princess Snow White had ordered her immediate execution and no more would she conduct her reign of terror over the land.

The people rejoiced.

Snow White was made Queen and after asking Cornflower for her hand in marriage, crowned her as Queen Consort.

Though they did not live happily ever after, they remained together till death and were still very much in love with one another by the end.

Quite the achievement, all things considered.

Golden Eyes

Part IV

With every passing day, the birdsong got louder.

*I*t reached such a cacophony of mangled wailing that Golden Eyes was often at a loss trying to pretend she did not hear them. Hearing them meant the Goblin King's magic was failing. Should he find out, he would once again cast his befuddling enchantment and have her forget the existence of time and the presence of a world outside his. It was most upsetting.

But she persevered.

Until one day, Golden Eyes could stand it no more.

Early in the night, she crept into the clearing, basked in moonlight. She knelt as if she were in preparation to worship the Goddess. Her hands tied in supplication before her and she whispered:

"Tell me what to do. I beg of you. I want to help."

The answer she received was not a clear one. Neither was it given in any known mortal language. But after living amongst the trees, wild and unrestrained for so long, Golden Eyes understood. The birds could still not be seen, except a shimmer in the air here and a flash of a beady eye there. But their instruction was succinct and their supplication desperate.

The Goblin King perceived a change in Golden Eyes after that night.

And she perceived a change in him.

The iridescent golden of her eyes was a burnished amber now. It no longer shone bright. She had a taste for berries that destroyed her desire for his cooking. She walked through the woods at night, lips stained with the red of the sour fruits, and eyes glittering with malice. Her red cloak was in tatters and her red shoes worn out.

Often, he would play games with her.

"Fly, little bird, and I will hunt you and bring you back home."

"This is not my home," she would whisper, sinking deeper into his choking embrace.

And he would say – savouring each word –

"This is your home, for you have no other."

And she was lost again.

That morning, as the Goblin King lay half asleep with his head in her lap, Golden Eyes looked out of the window. There, cage upon cage, hung in a waterfall of iron and ivy, hanging from one side of the clearing. All were occupied, except for one. It took pride of place at the front, its little door hanging open. Waiting.

The cages, they cast such a shadow, the sunlight mattered no more. His spell was lifted and she saw the canker it disguised underneath.

For the first time, the birds were silent.

They looked to her, a gravity in their eyes that weighed her down, a thousand balls of iron crushing her soul.

"Wait for me," she murmured.

And then she continued to brush his hair through. A single white strand came free from his scalp and she wrapped it around her finger, a silken thread. A noose. Her finger bulged, reddening. As she brushed, she began to sing to the tune of his flute. Soft and sad.

"Once he has you, he keeps you.

He destroys you, he skins you, he leaves you out to dry.

The Goblin King is worse, much worse than the devils of old."

She grabbed two great tufts of his downy hair and she wrapped it around his throat. And then she strangled him. He did not wake. The night before they had plied one another with the most potent of wines, except hers had watered the earth and not her throat. The Goblin King slept through his death and was none the wiser.

She let him fall to the ground in a slump and went outside to the clearing. One by one, she released the birds from their cages and a most marvellous thing began to happen. The birds turned into young men and women, mortals in the primes of their lives, for time had ceased to ravage them after their imprisonment. On the throat of each, a bite of lust, that matched the one on hers. A perfect imprint of the Goblin King's teeth marring their lovely, tender flesh.

Golden Eyes watched them run free, so joyous, so eager. Very soon they would be faced with horror and grief as they realised the world they craved for had left them behind. But they would not return to these woods. They would go anywhere they could, but never here. And so, Golden Eyes thought nothing more of it.

She remained in the woods. She could not leave.

For the Goblin King had left more than a tender love mark on her throat.

The seed that grew in her belly was his revenge.

It tied her to the forest. It made her feet burn like hot coals if she tried to leave.

Golden Eyes lived in the Goblin King's lair till the day she died.

Beauty and the Beast

*O*nce upon a desolate time, famine struck a bountiful land. Plague followed quickly on its heels, and those who had not died from hunger, suffered in the ravages of illness. Misery settled over the land for months on end with no signs that it would get any better.

Some blamed it on the deceased mother of the Queen. She had been a witch and it was now common knowledge that she had been adept at curses. Other blamed it on Queen Snow White herself. She was old and ailing now and had no heir. She had lost the woman she dearly loved, her wife, and was said to be a cantankerous recluse who refused to leave a chamber. Some said it was built behind a mirror, though no one quite knew why.

It was quite a hopeless situation really.

And none more so than in the once thriving town of Hamlin.

It was known as the cherished birthplace of the late Queen Consort, the Most Honourable Lady Cornflower. Snow White had always favoured the town and often stopped by every winter solstice with her wife. It increased the number of visitors to Hamlin by the year, bolstering its coffers with the gold they spent, until finally, it was named the most glorious place to live in the entire kingdom. The plagues of old were but a fading nightmare, as was the tale of the dastardly Pied Piper that had once haunted the streets of Hamlin.

But the town's short-lived glory was over and it sank to the ravages of famine like the rest of the land.

A certain merchant who had once ruled a thriving empire built off of the spice trade was just one of the rich residents Hamlin who had been brought low. His opulent mansion had been replaced by a cottage and his army of

servants by an elderly gardener and a starving guard dog. He had three sons, but two were of no use to him. They had been raised in luxury and had expected to marry well and never work a day in their lives. They would not start sacrificing pride for the purposes of feeding their hunger now. The youngest was a different story altogether.

He had a birth name but his mother had always called him 'Beauty' and the nickname had stuck. And truly, he deserved it. He was not flaxen haired like his brothers and instead had hair the colour of dark chestnut. But it was his eyes which his mother had named him for. They were so dark they were almost black and there seemed to be an eternal light in their depths. In sadness and in happiness, Beauty's eyes shone and enamoured the hearts of all those who looked upon his face.

Beauty was a young child when misfortune struck. His mother died within the same year and he became very attached to his father. He did not remember growing up with toys, or having food aplenty and wardrobes filled with clothes. Unlike his brothers, he had never ridden horses, gone hunting or indeed done any of those activities which the rich were so fond of. Indeed, he did not care that he had not. He was content with the magic tricks he devised and performed, much to the delight of the street urchins that often milled around the house.

Beauty liked his life in the little cottage with both his brothers, as stingy and as miserable as they might be. He had enough love in his heart to share and he did not mind that they did not reciprocate even a jot of it. Besides, he had no such complaint about his father.

The old merchant decided he would travel far from Hamlin with his wares and sell them in the neighbouring land. Very few people in Hamlin had gold to exchange for his dwindling supply of spices and he was becoming desperate.

Before he left, he asked each of his three sons: "What is it that you would like me to bring back for you upon my return?"

The eldest answered, "I'd quite like to have a new fencing sword, father. My old one is quite tarnished." When his father was surprised and asked why (for fencing was the last of anyone's worries in the current climate and wouldn't he rather have a sturdy broadsword?) he said, "Goodness father! Does keeping up appearances mean nothing to you? You may have forgotten where we come from but I assure you, *I* have not!"

The second son answered, "I want a new waistcoat and as many powdered wigs in the latest fashion as you can find, father. And perhaps a spot of rouge?"

The merchant decided not to question him.

And finally, Beauty answered, "A rose, father."

To this, the old merchant smiled quietly, his eyes filling with tears. He caressed his youngest son's cheek and said not a word, for he knew why Beauty had asked for such a simple thing.

It took him many weeks to return, but when he did, winter had come to Hamlin. Glimpses of the yellow brick road peered through an expanse of glittering, crisp snow. It veered around the town and continued into the distance, stretching as far as the eye could see. The merchant steered his horse off onto a smaller path headed straight for the town. He was most perturbed. He had found each of the things his oldest two sons had requested. And yet, he had not been able to acquire a single rose for Beauty.

He was so deep in thought, he did not notice that the horse had veered off the path and was now merrily trotting towards a large expanse of forest to the east of Hamlin. The animal trotted fast, sprightlier than it had been in years. It appeared to be under some mysterious influence, its eyes rolling as it frothed at the mouth. When the old merchant

attempted to steer it around, it neighed wildly and then charged deeper into the thicket of trees. The old man was quite frightened now as the weather started to take a turn for the worse.

A most terrible wind roared its anguish over the barren treetops, lashing their branches to and fro. They groaned, a macabre orchestra of wood upon wood to add to the wind's howl. Snow began to fall, blinding the merchant and soaking his ragged coat. He was shivering from head to foot by the time the wind finally quieted. His horse slowed to a canter and the man looked around, searching desperately for a familiar path. But he had never been this deep into the forest. For good reason too.

There had always been whispers about the strange creatures that inhabited the darkness of these woods. Not faeries, not goblins, but something infinitely worse. In some cases, it was said the forest itself inspired such fear. It stretched over the border into the neighbouring land, knowing no bounds and heeding the territories of no man. It was a living creature in and of itself.

The old merchant was quite frightened now, for night had fallen and he saw no way out. He felt he must starve and freeze to death. What a miserable fate!

He got down to the ground, intending to spend his final hours in prostration to the Goddess, praying to Her to protect his children and what little he had left for them. Even his last thoughts revolved around his three boys, his most precious jewels.

But as luck would have it, the Goddess smiled kindly upon the old merchant that day and decided he would live to see another.

It was the horse's nervous whinny that made him look up. And there, lo and behold, in the near distance…lights!

The merchant climbed back onto his horse and urged it on. The lights sparkled clearly through the gloom and he wondered if he was seeing things at first. His heart pounded in his ears, a marching drumbeat, accompanying him all the way up to the iron gates of a magnificent house.

"My goodness," he murmured in astonishment.

How had such a house come to be built in the middle of such a wild forest? Its architecture was dazzling, built in the fashion of the palaces of old. If he tried, he would have counted a hundred windows and that was only in the front. The snow fell slower and softer now and the air was still.

The merchant got off his horse and walked ahead on foot, leading his animal behind him. He pushed at the gates, expecting them to remain firm. But one gave way and he walked through. He was tense, expecting at any moment to be accosted by some fearsome creature, some strange thing of the dark. For though the house was beautiful, there was something not quite right about it.

But hunger and weariness won out and he did not turn back.

As he walked through the sumptuous gardens, he was most surprised to see that the flowers on the hedges and in the ground, were in full bloom despite the thick coating of winter snow. It convinced him there had to be some ghastly magic afoot. It was not natural.

Upon seeing a tall bush covered in red roses, the merchant paused.

"A rose, father."

His youngest child's voice sounded in his ears and he felt his heart plummet. He so wished to return and see the smile on Beauty's face when he brought him his desired gift. With sweat beading on his forehead, the merchant drew closer to the bush. He lifted a trembling hand and –

The front doors to the house swung open, swathing him in a golden pool of light. He decided he would return to the rose bush later and went about finding a stable to put his horse in. He found an entire array of them, though they

appeared to be empty. Whoever owned the

house had to be the owner of great wealth and his curiosity was growing with each passing second.

But the merchant did not have the pleasure of seeing his host that night.

Food was laid out on the table in the grand dining hall and he waited a while, wondering who would come to eat it. He intended on asking permission before taking a bite or two. But when no one appeared, he eyed it longingly. It would get frightfully cold soon. In the end, he sat down and did not just take a bite or two. He gulped down as much as he could, his stomach receiving its best meal in many moons. As he ate, somewhere in the distance, a violin strained with the weight of melancholy notes, strung together in one long aching symphony of regret.

And when the merchant was done, he was too tired to search for a place to rest in the house. Instead, he put his head on his arms and fell asleep right there at the table.

Some hours later, the sunlight welcomed him to the dawn of a new day. The table had been cleared away and before him sat a breakfast tray, laden with new dishes and a steaming pot of tea. The merchant was quite delighted, wondering what marvellous servants they must be that had gone about their business without so much as making a sound.

After having a hearty breakfast, the merchant went about the house, exploring. Most of the doors were locked but a few were open, including one that led into a vast library. He thought of Beauty once more and how the boy would love to be here amidst this treasure trove of knowledge. He went further in until he found a desk and some parchment and quills in the drawers. An ink bottle sat waiting and after a moment's thought, he penned a simple thank you to the owner of the house.

And though there was a heaviness in his heart at the thought of it, he started directing his footsteps back out of the house. He retrieved his horse, which was quite sated by the buckets of hay and oats that had been in the stable, and rode it back down the winding garden path. When he passed the rose bush, the merchant reached out and plucked one.

As soon as its stem snapped, a shadow fell over the grounds of the mansion. Thunder clapped in the clouds above and it was suddenly dark as night. He heard the frightfullest shriek, an unearthly sound that made his horse bolt in terror, flinging his rider off his back. The merchant curled up on his knees, cowering.

"Who dares steal from the daughter of the mighty Erl King?"

The ground shook, as a mighty pair of boots crashed down upon it. He looked up, quaking and sobbing under his breath. Towering over him stood a monstrous woman with flowing snowy white hair, fangs that reached her chin and irises of flashing gold with slit pupils. He thought her to be a woman for she had a feminine figure despite its size, but she was like no woman he had ever seen. He knew this was a creature of Hell that stood before him. And she had uttered the name of a demon that would send shivers down the spine of the bravest man. If she was his daughter, the merchant felt he was doomed.

"Rise, wretched human!" she spat, stamping her foot in anger.

He grovelled and attempted to do so. But his legs, traitors that they were, refused to allow him to stand. He fell twice before finally, her clawed, hooked hands yanked him upright.

"My lady, forgive me for my transgression!" he wailed, rubbing his palms together in a pathetic plea. "I was hungry and lost and had forsaken all hope of life! The lights of your blessed house seemed to me a haven of safety and comfort! I tried to find who owned such a wonder but to no avail! Allow me to offer my deepest apologies – "

"Silence!"

Her voice roared, shaking the forest around it for miles. He could not have spoken further if he'd wanted to. It was as if he were struck dumb upon her merest command. She stared at him, breathing hard. The air rattled through her lungs, sounding like a growing avalanche in the mountains. Her tail lashed the earth as she drew forward. A single talon touched the rose he still had clenched in his hand. Though his hand shook, he held on tight.

"Foolish mortal," she sneered, "I care not what you ate from my table or how long you stayed. However, your entitlement disgusts me. How dare you think you could leave my gates and take something of mine without my permission?"

"B-but, my lady, it is but a poor rose, the dearest wish of my youngest son. I did not think – "

"Does this look like any other rose to you?" she snarled, striking him across the face.

He lurched against the hedge, catching his balance in time. But not before the thorns slashed him like a hundred tiny nails. The Beast glared at the rose in his hand, but her demeanour was quite changed now. She seemed calmer, more composed.

"You have a son?" she said.

"Y-Yes, my lady, I have three. But the youngest is dearest to me. Love for him drove me to commit such a heinous offence as theft from the one who so generously hosted – "

"Shut up."

The Beast paced back and forth, running her talon over her crusted lips. After a few minutes of thought, she turned to him and grinned.

"For how much you love him, tis a shame you must leave the world without bidding him goodbye," she said. "You must give your life in exchange for your crime."

"My lady!" the merchant fell to his knees once more. "If I must die, let the blow fall heavy and quick! But if I may beseech you, allow me to see my sons one last time! May all the curses in the land befall me should I break my promise and fail to return for my execution!"

"I will do you one better," she purred, "bring me your youngest son and I will spare your life. He will live with me in this house till the end of days. He will be clothed, he will be fed and he will be happy. Surely, you would wish such a thing for your beloved?"

He looked up at her with pitiful, tear-drenched eyes. "My lady, I would never see him again."

"That will be the price you pay in exchange for sparing your life," she answered. "Choose, mortal. Your death and your son living a life of abject poverty and strife. Or living till the end of your days and your son living to the end of all days."

The choice was most apparent to the Beast. But alas, she was not mortal. She knew not the pain in a parent's heart of never seeing one's child again. But for the sake of his Beauty, the merchant bowed and swore to abide by his oath.

The Beast clapped twice and within the blink of an eye, the merchant was standing at the gates of Hamlin with his horse beside him. With slow, trudging footsteps, he walked through. He wept bitterly until he reached his house. Then, he wiped away his tears and smiled bravely, not wanting to taint the joys of reunion with his boys.

They were all well-pleased with his gifts, especially Beauty who marvelled that a rose with a plucked stem should still look so alive and smell so fresh. He asked his father's permission to plant it on his mother's grave and the old man agreed. He accompanied his youngest son there for the purposes of revealing the heavy price that the rose had exacted.

Beauty was astonished to hear of his father's adventure and in turns, was both delighted and mystified. But by the end of his tale, his face was quite green and he looked as if a ghost had trapped him in its cold embrace.

"Look not so miserable, my son," the merchant said kindly, touching his cheek, "I will not allow you to go to such an evil place. I have made up my mind. I will return within the month and offer up my life."

"No, father, no," Beauty said quickly, "I will not allow you to do such a thing. Besides, you gave her your oath that you would take me. What if she exacts vengeance and kills us all? She must be a demon for only the Erl King's children could have such power. She could raze Hamlin to the ground."

And he would hear nothing more of it.

Beauty made all his preparations in the next month. He handled unfinished business with friends and worked twice as hard at the blacksmith's shop to earn enough money to leave to his father. He kept himself distracted, for should his mind wander, he would begin to imagine what horror the Beast must be and what fate awaited him in the haunted corners of the forest.

When the day of reckoning arrived, he woke at the crack of dawn and set out. Goodbye was far too painful and Beauty knew his father's tears would shake the courage he was holding onto with such difficulty.

Alone, Beauty made the journey eastward to the forest. He remembered how his father had mentioned a freak snowstorm hitting as soon as he set foot in the undergrowth. Upon walking a few yards in, he felt the air become colder. The wind struck up its haunting symphony and just like his father before him, Beauty felt he was going to be eaten alive by the rage of the storm. And some distance away, he thought he heard the muted clopping of a horse's hooves, trampling the sandy surface of the yellow brick road beneath them. Except the road was miles away.

Just when he thought he could bear no more, it stilled and he spied lights in the distance.

Upon laying eyes on the grand old house, Beauty forgot the sadness swirling in his stomach. In fact, he forgot everything as he stared in awe. Unlike his father, he did not immediately follow the direction of the scent coming from the dining hall. Instead, he called out, announcing his arrival. If he had to face this fearsome Beast, he would see her now whilst his stomach was empty and he would not heave up its contents.

But in answer, he got nothing, except the plaintive echoes of his own voice.

It was a haunted house.

Nothing stirred, though the candelabras were all lit and the hearths ablaze with heat. He tried to open locked doors only to be distracted by ones that creaked ajar seemingly on their own. He hurried to try and catch the culprit but was only faced with more stony silence. It was enough to make a boy mad, walking the long, marbled halls and seeing or hearing no one. Nothing but the far away strains of a violin, mournfully playing arias to accompany his wild goose chase.

Finally, he had had enough and he descended the grand staircase to find the dining hall.

After eating his fill – the first good meal he had had in months – Beauty went upstairs once more, hunting out a bedroom he had seen earlier. He put down his small bag of worldly belongings and fully meant to return outside and explore the grounds further. But all it took was one hand to rest on the silken, plush bedding for his eyelids to droop.

"Just a short nap," he said to himself with a languorous yawn.

And then he climbed onto the bed and as soon as his head touched the pillow, he was fast asleep.

The flames of the candles flickered and were snuffed by an unseen hand.

When Beauty awoke, the silence still hung thick. But he felt an uneasy, crawling sensation on the back of his neck. Something had woken him up against his will. He sat up, rubbing his eyes and blinking away the fogginess in his vision. The lights were out but the door was ajar, letting in enough of a glow from outside to see that the room was empty.

Beauty got out of bed and walked out into the hallway. High above, through circular glass domes on the ceiling, moonlight poured in, ribbons of silver wrapping around him. He smiled, feeling strangely light and wandered down the corridor as if in some waking dream.

"What a beauty you are…"

Beauty froze as he heard the soft voice dance around, whispering in the throes of a breeze that had no origin and no end. The windows were all closed and yet his hair fluttered in the gust of cool air.

The voice belonged to that of a young woman. He had been expecting something rather different, something guttural and savage like his father had described. It was the house playing tricks on him, encouraging him to lower his guard. It had to be. But upon taking another step, the voice sounded again.

"Why do you walk away from me, my love? I am here! Come to me!"

"Where?" Beauty burst out, spinning around.

Someone had been behind him, he had felt it. But again, he was faced with an empty corridor. The voice began to sing, an ancient folk song, listing the many doomed lovers of the Erl King. It reached a pitch of utter despair when it sang of the last, the one with the golden eyes. Beauty did not heed the foreboding contents of the lyrics and followed the inviting melancholy of its sound, running through hallways and up and down staircases.

At last, he stopped before a door that was wide open.

Beyond lay a sumptuous bedchamber, awash with moonlight that sparkled through the windows, brighter than the glow of a hundred faeries. Beauty's thudding heart calmed and he drifted inside, his face in equal parts confused and enchanted.

"Where are you?" he whispered weakly, calling to the voice with no owner.

"Here."

He jumped as he felt warm breath heat the skin on his nape. When he turned, he began to retreat from the edge of madness. He was no longer alone.

A beautiful young woman stood before him, with a smile that made his heart come close to bursting. She was the most exquisite, fragile creature he had ever laid eyes on. Her snowy white hair fell to the ground in waves, mahogany skin glowing against it in startling contrast. But most of all, her eyes – oh, her eyes – as bright and as fiery as the sun. So golden were they, he knew instantly she was no mortal. And yet…

"You are…the Beast?" he said, puerile wonder marking his face.

She laughed, a sparkling sound, like the tinkle of glass beads on ice. She laughed with such gusto, throwing her head back and clasping her hands under her chin. She laughed like a little girl and it was endearing to watching.

"I see that it is to be my name. I quite like it," she smiled.

"I-I apologise, my lady. Your birth name must be as beautiful as yourself and I would be honoured to hail you by it. I know not what spell my father was under to mistake you for the hideous creature he described to me," Beauty stammered out.

"Fear not. Your father saw one of my forms, the one I choose to take when I am quite angry," the Beast replied sweetly. "I would not be half as imposing if I flew into a rage like this now, would I?"

She twirled around, her gauzy white dress floating around her.

She was a marvel. Beauty could not take his eyes off her. He quite believed, though he had never experienced the feeling before, that he was in love. And she in turn, was quite smitten with him.

The Beast would not allow him to return to his room, not that he even desired it. Instead, she took his hand and kissed it, inviting him to her bed.

Beauty suddenly became unbearably shy. He did not want to disappoint her. He certainly did not consider fumbling, giggling, heated encounters with the blacksmith's daughter in the dark to be proof of experience. And yet when the Beast kissed him, he forgot his insecurities. He tasted and felt only the magic of her wilful desire and passionate embrace.

She took him to bed and made him a man.

Beauty did not realise he still considered himself a boy until he looked up to see her astride him, the magnificence of her slender form being his to touch, to kiss, to hold. The hours fluttered away, lost to trembling limbs, fervent cries and ecstasy that rivalled all the other pleasures of the world. Such was the lust coursing through his veins, Beauty could not bear to let her go even when she whispered that she was tired. He was alive with all the eagerness of a young buck and he was at it again. She obliged him one last time, her breathless laughter resounding in his ear as he sobbed into her shoulder from the overindulgence of physical delight.

At last, he too was worn out and fell onto the soft down of her bed, the sweat on his skin cooling and his chest heaving. He had quite forgotten to breathe for a while there and it was as if he were teaching himself how to do so for the very first time. It was not long before he began to give in to the clutching embrace of sleep.

He was not quite upon the threshold of slumber when he felt her on top of him once more.

"My lady…" he murmured, not sure if this were a dream.

She did not answer him.

Beauty felt a cold pinprick on his chest and his eyes began to force themselves open. He looked up just in time to see the Beast marking a spot on his smooth breast with a dagger. Then she lifted her arms, holding the terrifying point high above her head. Before she could bring the dagger down, her eyes met his.

Beauty lay still, gazing at her with such softness in his eyes that she faltered.

"My lady," he whispered. "I could not wish for a sweeter death."

"Are you naïve or just easily defeated?" she said. "You stare death in the face with a smile. That is not the way of mortals."

"I would have died soon enough in Hamlin," he answered. "By plague or by famine or simply bad luck. Never would I have dreamt that I would get to spend my final day and night in such luxury, having been in the arms of such a lovely creature. I know you are not human, but that does not matter to me. For I have fallen in love with you, my lady."

The Beast lowered the dagger, a scathing laugh ripping from her lips. "Foolish boy, what do you know of love?"

"I know that I love you," he said simply.

"I am the daughter of a demon and you would do well to know that."

"You could be the mother of a hundred demons and I would not alter my words."

"Foolish boy!"

With this last exclamation, the Beast leapt off the bed, landing lightly on her two feet and flinging the dagger aside. She went to the window, throwing back the curtains

and turning her golden eyes up towards the starlit sky. The fire of dawn had not yet begun to burn. The air was filled with that sombre, sweet stillness preceding the rise of the sun. A tear rolled down the Beast's face and her frail shoulders shook with repressed sobs.

Beauty sat up slowly. Her slender profile did not do well to disguise her crying, though her lips clamped like a vice to keep all sounds caged behind them.

"My lady, have I upset you?" he asked.

"No! No, you have not, you well-meaning fool!" she exclaimed, letting the dams burst forth and sobbing with her whole heart.

Beauty did not understand the reason behind her tears. But he recognised their pain and that was all that mattered. He walked up behind her and wrapped her in his strong, warm embrace. He rested his cheek on her head and stroked her hair, whispering words of sweet comfort in her ear. The Beast quite forgot who she was for a moment as she allowed herself to sink against him. No man had ever touched her like this. Indeed, she had not allowed any man to. His hand was heavier and larger, but the way it smoothed through her hair, reminded her of her days as a little girl when she had rested her head in her mother's lap, wanting her hair brushed.

Her mother with eyes as golden as hers, the killer of her father and the only mortal being the Beast had truly loved.

"I am a most horrendous creature, Beauty. And you will soon see," she whispered. "Come, I must show you something."

She took him down underneath the great house, to a catacomb that led into a huge cavern. Its rock walls glowed with an unearthly red glow and from floor to ceiling, they were lined with golden rings. Each ring was outlined by a square. They were drawers, fitted into the rock, covering

every inch of it. There must have been hundreds.

The Beast pulled open the first and inside, crystallized in amber, was a little sparrow.

"This is how I remain young and beautiful," she told him. "This is what you would have become, Beauty. A little bird encased in a shelf underground. I cannot leave this forest, just like my father. And like the Erl King, I must feed my immortality and my youth with the willing sacrifice of others. These are all young men and women, victims of my seduction, doomed to remain forever entombed. But you - I became impatient with you. I was of a mind to kill you quickly lest I - I lose the heart to do so. Now....do you still love me, Beauty?"

She asked the question with a poignant, mocking air.

And Beauty's response served to befuddle her once more.

"Yes," he said simply, "for I stand here with you and not slashed at the heart by your dagger."

"How can you see the evidence of all my heinous immortality and still have the gall to say you love me?" she exclaimed in horror. "You are but a deranged young fool after all!"

Beauty took her hand, ignored her agitation and kissed it.

"Fear not," he said kindly. "I am as sane as any other young man in love. But I see things not even your immortal eyes perceive. I see that you are regretful of the heinous acts you have had to commit to stay alive. Perhaps out of compulsion to be like your father, I know not. But you would not have spared me if you truly wished to go on like this."

"You do not understand. I must capture youth after youth to remain immortal! Else I will die like my mortal mother!" she cried. "I have spared you, but I will not spare the next!"

"But you can. You can release the birds and turn them back into their former selves. And then you can live to grow old with me. Surely, moral life is not such a great price to pay if one can live through it with happiness?"

Beauty's fingers interlaced with hers and the smile on his face made her deadened heart beat faster than it had in many years. His promise was so ingenuous and yet so enticing.

"We shall live together as Beauty and the Beast till the end of our days. Though I fear our names are ill suited and should be reversed," he said, laughter dancing merrily in his kind, dark eyes.

She pulled her hand from his, a single tear rolling down her cheek. His heart faltered. But then, she turned and lifted her hands, muttering a torrid, quiet enchantment. The foreign words rumbled through the room. The ground began to shake and with it, all the shelves holding their hundreds of captives.

The Beast willed herself to do the spell correctly, just the way her mother had taught her. She envisioned the little birds becoming human again, young boys and girls, free to escape. But something was wrong. Her magic felt laboured, not effortless like Golden Eyes had said it should be. Her hands shook and she felt a terrible stab of pain in her heart.

Beauty ran towards her in alarm upon hearing her cry, but she held him back with one hand, keeping him anchored with a spell.

"You cannot stay here! The spell is not working, you will be killed!" she screamed.

"No! I won't leave you!" he yelled over the roar of the quaking ground.

But as the ceiling began to disintegrate, the Beast cast one final spell with all the might left inside her. It banished Beauty from the forest, far, far away. Somewhere safe.

And she was left alone to face the retribution of the terrible curses she had cast over the years. The birds were

lost to her, the humans they had once been were now long dead. But the magic entrapped inside each escaped and backfired on its caster, raining down upon her with a terrible vengeance.

The Beast's house crumbled to the ground in one fell swoop. The gardens wilted and shrivelled, merging in with the wild undergrowth of the surrounding forest. The trees closed in, jealously encroaching on the space they had been forbidden to draw near for so long. Within moments, all signs that a house had ever been there, had vanished.

And under the ground, the Beast shrieked in terror as her reversed spells destroyed her from the inside out.

They did not kill her. But the agony she felt was akin to dying.

With no power left inside her, she clawed her way out of the cavern with her bare hands. It took her days, without water, without food, before she managed to pierce the surface of the earth. A hand emerged, scrabbling in desperation, followed by the rest of her. There, in the light of day, the aftermath of the curse became apparent.

From head to toe, her skin had turned green. Her white hair was wild and tangled with dirt and leaves. Her dress was muddied and torn. Was this what it felt like to be mortal? This disparaging weakness of body and mind? She felt as if she were on the verge of tears as she looked at her green hands and arms.

The wind blew the skirts of her dress back and the glint of red on her feet made her look down. As the Beast sobbed and wiped her face clean of tears, she gazed at her mother's last gift with renewed focus. The pretty red shoes that her father had gifted to his final conquest, not realising that she would never return them, for she would not fall prey to his wiles. Her mother's voice sounded, as if through a large body of water, whispering the words that had accompanied the precious gift:

"When you are at your most helpless, click the heels of these shoes together three times and think to yourself...there's no place like home. And I promise you, Elphaba, you will find your way."

She had never done as her mother had said for she had never felt lost. But now, she once again felt like a small, bewildered girl, afraid to walk deeper into the forest without her mother's guiding hand upon her back. Closing her eyes, she took a deep breath.

She clicked her heels thrice.

And thus, she found herself standing on the famed yellow brick road, her direction facing westward. By the roadside, sat a wizened old beggar with a black horse tied up to a post beside him. They paid her no mind, not at all surprised to see her appear out of thin air.

As if of their own volition, her ruby-clad feet began to walk, taking her onwards. She had never been outside of the forest her entire life. Immortality had certainly not blessed her with everything. There was a sense of renewed excitement inside her and her pace quickened, eager to find what lay at the end of the yellow brick road.

As for Beauty –

Well, as far as I know, Elphaba's spell did not return him to Hamlin. He found himself in a small village in a neighbouring kingdom where he spent his days working as a blacksmith, and his nights as a magician performing wonderful tricks for enthusiastic parlour audiences. In fact, his repute grew so greatly that he became famous far and wide, many flocking to see his performances. It was not long before he decided he would expand his horizons and set his sights on a greater prize.

It was a city, an emerald city, not far from the village, that boasted an audience bigger and more splendid than any he had ever had before. There, he would make his name and there, awaited a glorious future. Now this city, was the capital city of the land of -

What was it again?

Its name...

Oh dear, what was its name? Something with an 'O'?

I do believe it has quite slipped my mind.

Publishers Note

I hope you enjoyed reading Twisted Tales. This is the first book that I have published and is the first book for Ms. Yasin also. I must say it has been a pleasure working with her.

Unfortunately due to unforeseen circumstances there may be a considerable delay before another edition from her will be available. Her next book may be delayed for some time. I hope the delay won't be too long.

Books in progress include another edition of Twisted Tales and a fantasy series that promises to be even better than Twisted Tales.

If you would like to see more from Tinker Books Publishing™ Please sign up up and indicate your reading preferences at:

http://bit.ly/tinkerbooks_subscribe

About the Author

Aneesa Yasin is an author living in Yorkshire, the grandest county in the UK. Just a short distance away is Haworth, birthplace of the famous Bronte Sisters. She credits the auspicious location of her residence and a first time reading of 'Wuthering Heights' as one of the strongest reasons behind her love of writing growing up. After graduating from the University of York in 2017, she has turned all her energy towards fulfilling her two life long dreams: becoming an author and adopting a dog, a cat and a kangaroo.

{Note: She is an author! > Editor}